ONE DARK AND STORMY KNIGHT

by

HERMIONE MOON

DEDICATION

To Tony & Chris, my Kiwi boys.

CONTENTS

Chapter One

The crack of thunder is so loud it makes me jump.

"Goodness," Delia exclaims. "That was right overhead."

"They did promise thunderstorms this evening." I walk across the café to the big front windows and look out at the view. "For once, the forecasters got it right."

A flash of lightning illuminates the ruins of Glastonbury Abbey. It's March seventeenth—St. Patrick's Day, and the clocks don't go forward for another ten days, so at 5:45 pm it's nearly dark, and it's raining heavily, too. Once the lightning fades, the Abbey descends into gloom.

I blink. I'm sure I saw a figure on the lawn in front of the Lady Chapel. Oddly, the person was standing still, unmindful of the atrocious weather. The lightning flashes again, and I peer at the murky scene, but the figure has vanished. I shrug and turn away.

"We might as well close," I advise Delia. This morning she told me she'd put a chicken in her slow cooker before she left for work, and I know she wants to get the roast potatoes on before her husband gets home. "There won't be any more visitors to the Adventure tonight in this weather."

The Avalon Café is part of the Arthurian Adventure—an interactive journey back through time exploring the myth of King Arthur and the Knights of the Round Table. It's right next to the building housing Glastonbury's museum, its archaeology field unit, and the library. In summer, at Christmas, and during bank holidays, the place is packed with visitors. But now the kids have gone back to school, and it'll be quiet until their next half-term holiday.

"Okay," Delia replies. "The dishwasher's stacked and I've wiped down the tables."

I smile. "You've done an amazing job, as always."

"Aw," she says. "You work yourself to a frazzle. Someone has to help you out."

Delia's worked at the café for over five years. Although her hair is grey and she has wrinkles at the corners of her eyes, she isn't quite old enough to be my mother. However, since the death of my real mum six months ago, she likes to keep an eye on me.

"I put aside a rosemary focaccia for you." I push the wrapped loaf across the worktop. I know that the rosemary, topped up with a calming spell for the stomach, helps her husband's indigestion.

Her face lights up. "I thought they'd all gone. You do spoil me."

"I know it's Brian's favourite. Give him a kiss from me," I tell her.

"I will." She collects her raincoat, pulls up the hood, and waves goodbye. Then, the loaf tucked under her arm, she scurries out of the café. Thinking about the lone figure standing in the rain, I watch her run through the puddles to her car and wait until she drives away.

Finally, I turn back to the café, lifting some stray strands of hair that have come loose and tucking them into my messy bun. I think of Delia's hair and wonder when I'll first see grey in mine. I'm turning thirty in September, but so far, I haven't found any in my red hair. Mum had plenty of grey by the time she died in her fifties, though, so no doubt they'll start popping out soon.

There's not much more to do. I'll sweep the floor, clean the counter, and then I'll lock up and go home. I made a tray of small steak pies earlier today, and I saved myself one. I'll heat it up and have it with mashed potato and some green beans and finish off with a slice of my best chocolate cake.

I stop in front of the empty suit of armour that stands by the door, lick my finger, and clean off a smudge on the knight's breastplate. "There," I tell him, "all squeaky clean again." The suit belongs to the museum situated behind the Adventure, but it's stood here since I was a child, and I've always talked to him as if he's a real knight.

There used to be a separate kitchen in the café, but some time ago Mum made the decision to knock down the wall between it and the café and put glass in instead, as the customers like to watch the food being made, and it makes anyone working in there feel less isolated. I walk past the window to the break room where we eat our lunch and open the door.

The dog inside stands up as I open the door and wags his tail. "Hello, sweetheart," I say, bending to kiss his head. "You've been very patient, but everyone's gone. You can come out now."

Merlin appeared on the doorstep to the café a few weeks after my mum died. I don't know if someone left him there or if he'd always been a stray. He was certainly scruffy enough. He has a gorgeous face, long ears, and a light-brown curly coat. I'm not sure what breed he is; my best guess is a Labradoodle—a cross between a Labrador and a Miniature Poodle.

It was love at first sight on my part. I gave him a sausage and a hug, and promised to help him get back home. I put up posters and tried to find out where he lived, but nobody came forward to claim him. Every day he lay outside the café, and people soon grew used to seeing him there. Not wanting to leave him out at night, and after a bath and a trim of his curly hair, I started taking him home with me, and that was that—Merlin adopted me.

I say he adopted me and not the other way around, because he's not exactly tame. He refuses to wear a collar and leash. He still disappears during the day sometimes; I've never found out where, but he always comes back. He won't sleep on my bed, but lies in the hallway, at the top of the stairs, as if he plans to trip up any intruder in the night. I swear he understands what I'm saying, and his face is very expressive, like he's trying to talk back. And he always sighs when I put proper dog food in his bowl, as if he'd much rather have steak.

He trots past me into the café, and I pick up my broom and follow him. He sits and looks up at the mural on the wall opposite the door, and I follow his gaze. My aunt—my mother's younger sister, Beatrix—painted it. The picture shows King Arthur sitting on a horse, Excalibur in his hand, looking out over the Isle of Avalon, which many scholars think was located here, in Glastonbury. On the Isle, a woman stands with her hands raised, shrouding the Isle in magical mists. If you look closely, you can see that she bears a striking resemblance to the women in our family, with her long red hair tumbling to her waist, her bright green eyes, and her freckled nose and cheeks. It's not a coincidence. All the women in my family are witches. Beatrix added ground eggshell and snail shells to the paint before she began, and the picture holds a protection spell for the café.

"Yes, Mum," I say to the painting, as I do every night. "Out with the old, in with the new."

When Mum used to run the café, before she got too sick to work, the last thing she would do was sweep the tiled floor at night. Ostensibly it was to brush away the dust and crumbs, but for her it was also a spiritual cleanse, ridding the café of any negative energy it might have attracted during the day, and I've continued the tradition. The broom was hers, too, a proper witch's besom, made from twigs and herbs bound to a long pole. I've renewed the herbs a few times, but I'm sure it still carries some of her magic.

I switch on the radio and, humming along to the old folk song that's playing as the rain patters on the windows, I start brushing the tiles. I inhale with pleasure as the scent of lavender and rosemary from the broom rises to fill the café.

My back is to the door when it jangles, and I shiver as the cold breeze brushes across my neck. "The café's closed," I call, trying to reach beneath a chair for a cupcake wrapper that tumbled off the table.

"Surely you can make an exception for an old friend."

I straighten at the woman's voice and turn, my heart sinking at the sight of Liza Banks. Tall, slim, and beautiful, wrapped in a classy cream raincoat, Liza surveys me with the slight sneer she always seems to bear whenever she's talking to me.

"I need a cake for a celebration," she says. "I'm sure you have something I can use." Somehow, she manages to make it sound as if it's unlikely that anything I make would fit her high standards.

My first instinct is to tell her to stick her cake where the sun doesn't shine. My second is to fish out the two-day-old stale raspberry sponge from the rubbish bin, tidy up the frosting, and put it in a box for her.

But then my gaze falls on the witch in the painting, and I feel a twinge of guilt. Mum taught me that no matter how you feel toward a person, they should never be able to fault you on your politeness.

"Of course," I say, putting the broom aside. "Let me see if I can find you something."

I go behind the counter, conscious of Merlin still sitting by the painting, except now he's facing Liza. He's not growling, but I can tell from his expression that he disapproves of her. He's probably picking up on my irritation. I try to suppress it and concentrate on the couple of cakes that remain in the cabinet. The chocolate cake I was saving for tonight sits next to a lemon-curd sponge. I take out the lemon-curd sponge. I'll be polite, but I'm not giving her my chocolate cake.

"How about this?" I place it on the counter. "Fresh today, and the lemon curd is homemade."

"I suppose it'll do."

Gritting my teeth, I busy myself with taking out a flat cardboard box and clipping the sides together ready for the cake. "So, what's the big occasion?"

She gives me a smug smile. "I've got a new job."

4

"Oh?" I pick up the cake.

"I've been made Head Archaeologist at the Field Unit," she says.

I lower the cake into the box, then lean on the counter. For a moment, I'm so consumed with envy that I feel nauseous.

Liza and I went to the same high school. Liza was one of those cool girls who had everything. She was beautiful, with long straight blonde hair, she was rich and clever, and she was never short of boyfriends. I was tall and skinny with ginger hair, sticky-out teeth, and glasses, and Liza and her friends intimidated me. But despite this, for some reason I'm sure she was jealous of me. I think it was something to do with our shared love of history and archaeology. No matter how hard she worked, my grades were always a shade or two above hers, and I know that rankled.

She could have been a model, or an athlete, but she decided she wanted to be an archaeologist, just like me. At eighteen, we both went to the University of Exeter, and ended up in several of the same classes. Whilst doing her best to ignore me, Liza sailed through the first year, the life and soul of the party. But her grades remained steadily a fraction below mine, to her continued annoyance.

Eventually, braces straightened my teeth, contact lenses replaced the glasses, and my ginger hair took on gold highlights that some men appeared to find attractive, including a gorgeous history student called Luke Mathers, and we started dating. I was crazy about him for a while. But the rest of my life wasn't going so well.

My father died when I was young, and Mum was diagnosed with Multiple Sclerosis a few years afterward, so leaving her to go to university was hard for us both. The café wasn't making much money, so I existed on a pittance, and Mum's health gradually deteriorated. Halfway through my second year, it became clear to me that Mum could no longer cope on her own. Confined to a wheelchair, she was often too ill to run the café, and when she told me one day that she thought she was going to have to sell it, I knew I couldn't let that happen. Beatrix told me to stay at university and that she would help run the café and look after Mum, but Beatrix's art gallery was flourishing, and it didn't seem fair to make her give up her dreams. Against both their wishes, I left university and returned home.

A week later, Luke broke up with me. He said it was because traveling from Exeter to Glastonbury was too difficult, but I know it was because he didn't want to be with someone who had to look after a sick mother, because a week after he finished with me, he started dating Liza. I can't be sure, but I've heard that she made a beeline for him as soon as I left, and I know he'd never have been able to resist her charms. That was eight years ago, and they're married now. No doubt there will be beautiful babies on the way soon.

I'm nearly thirty, still single, and unlikely to tie the knot in the near future. But I'm not complaining. I don't resent their happiness. I don't want a man who won't stand by me when times are hard. And although I'd love to have been an archaeologist, I adore the café, and I'm content with my lot. I'm only human, though, and I do admit to feeling envy whenever I see Liza, who was immediately taken on by the Glastonbury Field Unit when she graduated, and who has obviously done a great job there, if she's been offered a promotion. She has everything a modern, successful woman could wish for.

I swallow hard, then close the lid on the cake box. Looking up, I meet her gaze. Her smug smile has spread—she's enjoying this.

"I'm very pleased for you," I tell her. As calmly as I can, I tell her how much she owes me. She takes out her money purse and counts out the coins, and I put them in the till.

"It's going to be amazing," she says. "It's just what I've always wanted—to head my own field unit. I knew you'd understand, because you had the same dream at one point, didn't you?"

"I did." I pass her the box.

She picks it up. "Well, I'm sure I'll be seeing you around. You know you're welcome to come over to the field unit anytime now that I'm in charge. We can always find something for amateurs to do."

"Goodbye, Liza," I say. "Enjoy the cake."

"We will. Luke loves lemon curd." She peers out at the rain. "I'd better go. I've got to call in at the library for something before I head home. I can't hang about; Luke can't bear to be without me in the evenings."

With a last, smug smile, she heads out of the café, leaving me with the lingering smell of her strong perfume, as the wind whips in and scatters the crumbs I've just swept up across the tiles.

Chapter Two

I watch her go, gritting my teeth. How come she can still get under my skin so easily?

I look down at Merlin. His eyebrows draw together.

"I know," I say. "She's not worth it, right?"

He comes over to me and nuzzles my hand, and I drop and put my arms around him. "I don't actually think I miss Luke," I murmur into the dog's curly fleece. "I miss the idea of him, you know? I mean, you're lovely, and you give really good hugs, but it's not quite the same."

He licks my face, and I laugh and kiss his nose. "All right. Let's forget about Liza and get on with sweeping the floor."

I collect the broom and continue brushing the crumbs into a pile, then use my dustpan and brush to pick them up and put them in the bin. Lastly, I take a cloth and go over to the counter to wipe it down.

That's when I notice the small money purse sitting in front of the card reader. It's Liza's. I pick it up. What should I do? I could lock it in the safe for the night, and hopefully she'll come back tomorrow to collect it. Then I remember that she said she was going to the library. I scowl. I don't owe her anything. It serves her right to be without her purse for the evening.

But once again, my gaze falls on the painting, and I sigh. "All right," I mumble, going through to the break room to collect my raincoat. "I'll be nice."

I pull it on and do up the buttons, pick up my umbrella, and walk back into the café. "Stay here," I tell Merlin.

He barks and jumps up at me. No doubt the storm is making him restless. "It's okay," I soothe, pushing him down gently. "I'll be back in a minute."

I walk past the knight and touch the pommel of his sword for luck, as I always do. Then I open the door and go out into the dark and stormy night. Merlin barks again, but I ignore him, pop the umbrella, and walk quickly along the path, past the entrance to the Adventure, toward the library and the field unit.

There's nobody about. Through the front window of the Adventure I can see Helen behind the reception desk, pulling on her coat, so she's obviously about to leave. The library's front doors are still open, though, as it's not quite six o'clock, and I go inside, shaking the drops off my umbrella and leaving it in the stand by the table with the vase of roses by the door.

The library is quiet and cool. Patience, the head librarian, is probably in the archives at the back. Everyone else is either in their offices or has already gone home.

I walk along the corridor that runs down the centre of the bookstacks, looking for Liza. Why did she come here? Maybe she needed a couple of reference books for one of the projects she was working on in her new role. Refusing to think about it, I call out impatiently, "Liza?" There's no reply, although there is a muffled sound from the reading room ahead of me, so I enter it through the open doors.

It's a large, circular room, with stairs up to a mezzanine floor that runs around the edge of the room, so anyone up there can look down on those studying quietly at the rows of desks. They're empty now, but I definitely heard something.

"Hello?" I call, walking forward through the desks. "Is anybody..."

I stop. Someone's lying on the floor in the centre of the room.

I inhale sharply. I can see slender bare legs, and long blonde hair fanned out on the carpet. She's wearing a cream raincoat. It's Liza. Her eyes are open, unseeing. There's an ugly red weal around her neck. With a shaking hand, I pick up her wrist and attempt to find a pulse. I fail.

She's dead.

I back up so hurriedly that I knock over a chair. My heart bangs against my ribs. Oh Goddess. I scan the room, breathing fast. It's only just happened; that means whoever killed her is probably still in the library.

Turning, I flee through the doors into the main library, and run along the corridor through the bookstacks.

I'm not thinking at all, just reacting. There's a bang behind me as someone knocks into a desk, but I daren't waste time by looking over my shoulder. I reach the front doors of the library, push open the doors, and run out into the wild and windy night.

I'm halfway back to the café before I remember my umbrella, but I can hardly go back now to retrieve it. All I can think of is that I want to get inside the café, where I always feel safe.

A flash of lightning splits the sky, followed immediately by a crack of thunder, and rain pelts down on my face, but I don't stop. I tear along the path, expecting to feel a hand on my shoulder at any moment, a knife through my ribs. I'm sure I can hear feet on the concrete behind me.

I reach the café door, throw it open, and run inside.

Merlin is barking furiously, but I run past him. I reach the counter, right as there's an almighty crash behind me. Startled, I stop and turn, just in time to see a figure fleeing back along the path.

By the front door, the suit of armour has moved. Normally, the sword in the knight's right hand is upright, leaning against his shoulder. Now, his arm is lowered, and the tip of the sword rests on the tiles. That's what made all the noise. Effectively, it blocked the murderer's entrance to the café, and it might even have hit him on the way down. He must have knocked into the suit as he came in and dislodged the knight's arm. How strange; the suit has stood like that for as long as I can remember. I'd assumed the arm was locked in place, maybe even rusted that way.

My chest heaves with my rapid breaths. My instinct is to flee, but I make myself wait and take in the scene. Merlin has dashed out of the open front door into the wet night, and he's now standing facing the direction of the fleeing person, barking furiously. The murderer has gone, for now.

I back up until I meet the wall, and stand there for a minute or so, trying to calm myself. When I feel confident he isn't coming back, I reach out a shaky hand and pick up my mobile phone from where it sits on a shelf behind the counter.

I don't even think of ringing 999. Instead, I dial my friend Imogen's number.

"Hello?" she answers after a few rings.

"It's me." I sound breathless, and I clear my throat and try again. "It's Gwen."

"Are you still at work?" she says. "You're a glutton for punishment in this weather."

"Can you come?" I ask. "There's… there's been a murder."

Imogen goes silent for a moment. Then she says, "What?"

"A murder," I repeat. "In the library. She's dead."

"Who's dead?"

"Liza Banks. She's in the reading room. I… I think she's been strangled."

"Where are you?" Imogen's voice is suddenly brisk and business-like. As a Detective Chief Inspector at the local police station, she's obviously learned to be calm in a crisis. I don't tend to see it much because she's ditsier than me where her personal life's concerned, but now I welcome her professional manner.

"In the café," I tell her. "I ran back. He followed me, and I think he was going to come in, but the knight saved me." I'm making no sense, but Imogen doesn't question me.

"All right," she says. "Lock the front door and stay put. Don't open it for anyone but a police officer, okay?"

"Okay."

"I'll be there as quickly as I can. And I'll call it in. Expect to see blue lights in a few minutes."

"Thanks, Immi."

She hangs up.

I put the phone down and walk across to the front door. "Merlin," I call. "Here, boy." He looks at me for a moment, then trots in. Quickly, I close and lock the door. Merlin shakes himself, spraying water everywhere, but I'm so relieved to have him by my side that I don't scold him.

I feel safer now the door's locked and Imogen is on her way. I look at the knight, take his sword arm, and lift it back into position. I'm not sure if I should leave it there, though—what if it falls on a customer? On a child? Maybe I should leave it lowered, instead. I try to pull his arm down, but it refuses to move. To my surprise it's locked in place again. How strange.

I look up at the knight's helm. It has a visor that's pulled down. The visor contains two narrow slits that would allow the knight inside to have a limited view of his surroundings.

Through the slits, a pair of blue eyes stares at me.

I squeal and back away, meeting the table behind me with a bang and almost falling over. I stare at the knight, my heart returning to its million beats per hour. I wait like that for a long, long time, staring at the visor. But the blue eyes have vanished, and the suit doesn't move.

Eventually, I move forward again to stand before him. Swallowing hard, I lift a hand to the helmet and raise the visor.

It's empty.

I lower it again, my head spinning. I must have imagined it. Obviously, there's nobody inside. It must have been a reflection of lightning in the window or something.

I'm sure it wasn't, but I ignore my gut feeling. I'm shocked, confused, disturbed by what I've witnessed. There's definitely a logical explanation.

The wail of police sirens begins in the distance. I move away from the knight and watch through the window as cars with flashing blue lights appear and park in the car park opposite. One pulls up right outside the Adventure, an ambulance tucking in behind it. Imogen gets out of the car, shouts directions to the police officers who swarm around her, and then she runs through the rain toward the café.

I unlock the door as she approaches, watching the suit of armour warily when she comes in, but the knight's arm doesn't move.

"Hey." Imogen's brown hair in its tight bun is wet and shiny, and it looks like melted chocolate. She's wearing a black raincoat over her navy suit. I met her on our first day at primary school. Another girl pulled my braids, so Imogen pushed her over, and she's been my guardian angel ever since.

She comes right up to me, holds me by my upper arms, and looks at my face. "Are you okay?"

I nod hastily. "I'm fine. A bit shaken up, but okay."

She scans me, as if checking for herself, then turns and greets Merlin, who's desperate for some fuss. "All right, boy," she says, stroking his ears. "Did you see off the nasty man?" He barks, and she chuckles. "Good boy."

She straightens and looks back at me. "Sit down. I'm going to put the kettle on and make you a cup of tea while you give me a statement."

So, she fills the kettle and puts a teabag into a mug, then takes notes while I tell her about Liza coming into the café, and what happened when I discovered she'd left her money purse behind. I explain how I found her body, and how I'm convinced someone chased me as I ran back to the café.

"So why didn't he follow you in?" she asks, passing me the mug when the tea is done.

I clear my throat. "The knight…"

Her expression softens. "What about the knight?"

Imogen knows I'm a witch. She's known since we were at primary school together and I first learned how to use spells in my baking. I made scones with herbs I'd blessed under a full moon with a spell to make you laugh, and I soon had the whole class giggling, including the teacher. Immi's fine with my magical talents, but I'm not sure that now is the time to confess anything other than the obvious.

"The person chasing me came into the café and bumped into the suit of armour," I tell her. "It knocked the knight's arm, and his sword fell down and frightened the murderer away."

"I thought Sir Boss was all rusted up," she states, going over to him. It's what we nicknamed him when we were very young after my gran showed us Bing Crosby in the movie version of *A Connecticut Yankee in King Arthur's Court*. Imogen tries to move his arm and fails. Frowning, she comes back to me.

"He is," I admit. "I don't know what happened. I lifted his arm and it stuck again, I swear." I feel a brief swell of panic that she doesn't seem to believe me. "Am I a suspect?"

There's a squeak from over by the door. We both look at the knight, who hasn't moved, then at each other.

"Of course not," Imogen says.

"I had a history with both Liza and Luke," I remind her.

"So did I, and I didn't do it." She waves a hand. "I've known you for twenty-four years. I think I can safely say you're not a murderer."

"I didn't like her," I confess, feeling an urge to be honest. "And I was jealous that she'd been given the role of head archaeologist. But I'd never harm her."

"Of course not," she repeats, "and we'll hear no more of that. Now, I'm going to ask an officer to stay outside the café while I quickly assess the scene, then I'll come back and we'll send you home. Okay?"

I nod. She rubs my arm. "You've had quite a shock," she points out. "It's going to be a stiff drink and an early night for you."

She smiles and goes out, and shortly afterward there's a police officer standing guard outside the door.

My gaze moves to the knight. The squeak of protest when I asked if I was a suspect was just the steel plates settling. The murderer banged into it when he rushed in after me and startled himself. The suit is empty.

But Merlin sits in front of it, staring up at the helm, and it's a long, long time before he finally looks away.

Chapter Three

"Gwen!" My aunt Beatrix stares at me with a mixture of delight and concern. "What are you doing here? Is everything okay?"

I stand on her doorstep and shove my hands in the pockets of my raincoat. "Not really." I shiver. "There's been a murder."

Beatrix is fifty-one, tall, and slender, like me. Her once-red hair is now completely grey, the fringe just showing beneath her colourful headscarf. There's a smudge of blue paint on her cheekbone—she's been in her art studio this afternoon. She blinks at my words. "I'm sorry, what?"

I take a hand out and rub my nose. "Can we come in?"

"Oh, Goddess, of course. You look soaked through. Max has lit the fire tonight. Go and warm yourselves."

I pass her into the hallway, unzip my jacket, and let her take it from me and hang it up on the peg by the door. Merlin follows me and shakes himself, looking rather miserable.

"Sorry," I apologize as he covers her and the walls with droplets.

"I'll get you both a towel. Go into the living room." She runs up the stairs.

I go in, and Uncle Max rises from his armchair and grins as Merlin runs over to him. Max is a couple of years older than Beatrix, and he has silver hair and a mostly white beard and moustache. He looks like Father Christmas. "Merlin! Come here and be hugged." He stops as he realizes the Labradoodle is soaking wet. "Oh! Ergh. That was a mistake." He looks up at me and his smile fades as he sees me shivering. "Gwen? You look frozen. Come and stand by the fire."

I can't stop my teeth chattering. "I th-think it's sh-shock."

"Why, what's happened?"

"I've j-just s-seen a m-murder."

He looks confused. "What, on TV?"

"N-no. At the l-library."

His jaw drops. "Bea," he says as she comes into the room, "Gwen says she's witnessed a murder."

"Definitely time for a stiff drink." Beatrix gestures at the cabinet behind him. He nods and takes out a bottle of brandy and pours a small amount into the bottom of a glass. "We can drive you home if you want," she tells me as she wraps me in a big thick towel. "Sit by the fire, love. Now, Max, can you make us all a cup of tea? And Merlin, come here and we'll try to get you dry."

Beatrix dries Merlin while Max makes the tea, giving me time to finish the brandy and gather my wits. I'm comforted by the familiarity of the room, with Beatrix's paintings on the walls—mainly of fantasy creatures like unicorns, angels, and mermaids.

When Max returns, I sit by the leaping fire and sip my tea while I tell them what happened, and within about ten minutes I'm warmer inside and out and my teeth have stopped chattering. Once Beatrix has rubbed his coat, Merlin comes and sits by my side, as if he's aware I need comfort. He rests his chin on my knee, and I scratch his ear.

"I still can't believe it." Max shakes his head. "Poor Liza. I mean, whatever we thought of her as a person, she didn't deserve to die."

"Poor Luke." Beatrix looks sad. She reaches out and squeezes my hand. "I'm so glad whoever did this didn't come into the café. I don't know what I'd do if lost you, too."

Beatrix took Mum's death hard. As witches, it's not often we feel powerless, but Mum's disease was well past any healing spell that either of us had the skill to cast. It was frustrating for Beatrix and me, but there's a saying amongst witches that not every broken blade is supposed to be mended. We have to accept that everyone has their journey, and it's not our place to change what's written in the stars.

"So, what stopped them going into the café again?" Max asked. "They knocked into the suit of armour?"

I hesitate. Max has no problem with the fact that his wife and her family are witches, but this might be a stretch, even for him.

"I'm not sure," I say carefully.

Beatrix narrows her eyes at me. "All right. Spit it out. What actually happened?"

I tell them how the knight's sword arm fell, and then when I lifted it again, it locked into place.

"Nothing unusual about that," Max says.

"That's not all. Afterward, when I looked at his visor… I swear I saw a pair of blue eyes looking back at me."

The two of them stare at me.

"Am I going mad?" I ask. "I mean, you know, barking?" Merlin snorts.

"Possibly not," Beatrix says slowly. "There are a couple of explanations. The Japanese have a word for it—*Tsukumogami*. They believe that any object that reaches its hundredth birthday may become alive and aware. Your suit of armour is medieval, isn't it?"

"It definitely dates back to the Reformation at least," I say.

"So maybe it's just, you know, taken on a life of its own."

"Maybe." I sip my tea thoughtfully.

"There's one other option," she says. "Most cultures have tales about inanimate objects that are inhabited by spirits, like Aladdin's genie in the lamp. In England, it's said that druids were once able to create something called a soulstone."

"A soulstone? What's that?"

"Apparently they could charm a precious gem to hold someone's soul. It was usually done as a curse, but there are also stories of it being done to save someone, until they discovered a way to put the soul back into a body."

"Like cryogenically freezing them?" Max says.

"Exactly."

"Wow." I don't know what to think about that.

"Do you want me to get a couple of lads to help move the suit out of the café?" Max asks. "Nobody wants a squatting poltergeist."

"I was frightened," I admit. "Initially. But I'm pretty sure he saved my life. Do you think that's possible?"

"Everything's possible." Beatrix smiles. "I think you should keep him. Every girl needs a knight in shining armour." Her eyes are gentle. She's worried about me. Since Mum passed, she calls in at the café most days to check on me.

"He's not very shiny," I joke to cover my emotion. "I think I need to give him a polish."

"I'm sure he'll enjoy that."

We all chuckle.

I finish off my tea. "I'd better go. I've interrupted your evening and kept you long enough."

"You can stay here tonight if you want," Beatrix says.

"Stay here?" I'm puzzled by her offer.

"If you're concerned about being alone," she clarifies.

She thinks I might be worried about the murderer coming to the house. That thought honestly hadn't entered my head. My stomach flutters—am I really in danger?

I shake my head. "I feel better for talking to you, but I'd like to go home."

"You should do a protection spell next time you do some baking," Beatrix says.

I nod. "I'll definitely do that."

"Want me to drive you home?" Max asks.

"I'll be fine. I've only had a couple of mouthfuls of brandy and it's not far."

I hug them both and they fuss up Merlin, and then I don my rain jacket and go back to my car.

The rain has eased up a bit, and I get home without too much hassle. I still live in the house I grew up in on the outskirts of town, as I haven't seen much point in selling up and moving when I love this place. I open the door, Merlin runs in, and I lock it behind us.

It's quiet, dark, and cold, and for a moment I regret leaving Beatrix and Max's house with its roaring log fire. I stand in the hallway, my heart banging on my ribs as I remember being chased by the murderer. He could be here, waiting for me…

But that's just fear talking, and I take off my jacket and boots, walk briskly along the hallway into the living room, and start preparing the fire. Within five minutes, the flames are eating up the kindling, filling the room with light and heat.

I know some people would find it depressing continuing to live in the family home after their parents died, but I love this room, with Beatrix's paintings on the walls, the shelves full of books on witchcraft that Mum and I collected over the years, the bowls of crystals and bottles of essentials oils, and all the other witch paraphernalia scattered around.

I go into the kitchen, which is my next favourite room. In the centre is a large pine table that belonged to my grandmother, on which she, my mum, and I have all kneaded dough over the years. Bundles of dried herbs hang from the ceiling, and the shelves are filled with hundreds of tiny jars of spices that I use in both my cooking and my spells, all blessed for different purposes—protection, love, wealth, happiness, health.

I tip Merlin's dog food into his bowl, roll my eyes at his sigh, then prepare my own dinner while he eats, filling the house with the smell of the warmed steak pie. I cook and mash some potatoes, heat up some green beans, and prepare a little gravy. When dinner's ready, I pour myself a glass of red wine, take it into the living room with my meal, and eat while I attempt to watch TV.

After a while, though, I put my plate aside and turn the TV off. Holding a second glass of red wine, I turn and lift my feet onto the sofa, dangling my free hand over the edge and burying it in Merlin's fleecy coat.

I think of Luke, who would know by now that his wife has been murdered, and wipe away the tears that run down my cheeks. I didn't like Liza; she wasn't a very nice person. But I didn't wish her ill.

My eyelids droop a little, and I finish off the last mouthful of wine. Unbidden, the memory of the pair of blue eyes rises in my mind. I think about the Japanese word—what was it? *Tsukumogami*, that's it. An object taking on a life of its own. Is that what's happened? The suit is so old that it's come alive? I slide down on the sofa a bit more. Something deep within me tells me that's not the case here. I think about Beatrix's explanation of the soulstone. Is it possible that someone's soul is captured in the suit?

I think of the genie in the lamp, and my joke to Beatrix and Max, *I think I need to give him a polish*, and my lips curve up in a smile.

For a moment, I worry about having bad dreams and reliving the moment when I found Liza. But I fall asleep quickly, and when I dream, it's about meeting a knight with startling blue eyes.

Chapter Four

"You're a Virgo, right?"

The question comes from Cooper, my chirpy, eighteen-year-old barista. He looks like a young Ryan Gosling, and I like having him in the café because I'm guaranteed to have a regular flow of young women coming in to order coffee, whether they actually drink it or not. He's in the middle of training at the local culinary college, and he works at The Avalon Café part time, gaining practical experience for his course. At the moment, there's a brief respite in the busy morning, and he's leaning on the counter, reading out our horoscopes on his phone.

"I'm on the cusp," I tell him as I collect the cups from a nearby table, smiling as I watch a child petting Merlin, who's sitting outside. "I was born at sunrise, when the Sun was moving from Virgo into Libra."

"All right." He consults his phone. "So for Virgo it says, 'This week you are liable to experience surprising events that upset your usual balanced equilibrium.'" He snorts. "They got that right."

"Just a bit." I bring the cups to the counter.

"It also says, 'Sexy Libra is super-hot right now, so if you're young, free, and single, you probably won't be for long!'" He looks up at me. "So you're going to witness a murder *and* fall in love. Sounds like quite a week."

"It certainly does." My hesitant smile covers the unease that has been there all morning. The Adventure, the library, and the field unit have been closed all morning while the police question everyone who works there and collect samples of everyone's DNA. SOCO—scene of crime officers—are coming and going, and we've been busy making coffees and muffins for the police. Imogen has been in a few times checking up on me and letting us know what's going on, as well as taking a statement. It's unsettling, and I miss the quiet normalcy of our daily lives.

The bell above the door sounds, and in comes Duncan, one of the archaeologists from the field unit, who also happens to be Cooper's dad. "Morning. Large mocha please, Coop. Two sugars."

"Coming right up." Cooper slides his phone into his back pocket and starts making the coffee.

"How are you doing?" Duncan asks me, looking over the top of his glasses. Everyone knows it was me who found Liza's body. They've all been keeping an eye on me throughout the day.

"Better now the sun's come out," I say truthfully. The storm has passed, and although it's not exactly warm, everything always seems better when the sun's shining.

"She's been baking," Delia tells him. "She always feels better when she bakes."

"We all feel better when Gwen bakes," Duncan says. "I'll have an apricot and cream cheese muffin with my coffee, please."

Delia bags it for him, and I smile as he pays. Apricots are packed with Vitamin A and Beta Carotene, which are great for eye disorders. I pop a little clear vision spell on them, and they're always popular with people with bad eyesight or eye problems, as well as helping them to think clearly when they've something important to do.

I do feel better when I'm cooking, if only because baking is the way I do magic, and doing spells invariably has an uplifting effect on the soul. Today I did what Beatrix suggested. Raisins are great at preventing many ailments and are perfect for a protection spell. I soaked some in a small amount of rum from a bottle that I'd left out under the light of a full moon, then used them in an oatmeal cookie mix, making sure I used the cinnamon I'd previously blessed for protection. Once the ingredients were all mixed in, I did the spell, asking the Goddess to surround whoever was eating the cookie with light, to keep them safe and protect them from harm. Once they were baked, I kept a few in an airtight box under the counter, and I've been breaking off pieces and nibbling them throughout the morning.

"Weather's definitely looking much better," Duncan says. He looks at his son, conscious, I think, that everyone's subdued today after Liza's death. "Want to drown a few maggots in the Brue later?"

Cooper nods. The two of them often go fishing together. "Friend of mine caught a twelve-pound pike yesterday."

"Cool. There's definitely a twenty-pound perch in there with my name on it. I'll pick you up at three?" He takes his coffee, waves, and goes out.

My buzzer sounds, so I go through to the kitchen and take out a new batch of feta and spinach muffins, put them aside to cool, and slide in some large sausage rolls. Allison and Joss, my two kitchen staff, are busy making sandwiches and filled rolls for the lunchtime rush. Everything is as it should be, and yet I still feel uneasy, with butterflies fluttering around in my tummy.

"Is Gwen around?" A man's voice sounds from the café. "I'd like to ask her some questions about how she found the murder victim."

I stop in the middle of lifting some cheese and bacon muffins out of their tin—cheese helps build healthy bones and teeth, and I throw a little happy spell on these to encourage people to smile. I know that voice. It's Matthew Hopkins. A local journalist, he's very proud of the fact that he's descended from the Witchfinder General who was responsible for the deaths of over three hundred witches in the seventeenth century. Channelling his ancestor's passion, he's writing a book about witchcraft in Somerset. He discovered that, in 1646, two witches were hanged near Glastonbury, and on reading that witchcraft passes down through the generations, he began researching the family trees of those two witches. And that's how he discovered that I'm descended from one of them, Alice Young. Apparently, I'm Alice's great, great, great… insert several more greats here… granddaughter. It doesn't help that my mother's name was also Alice, and her married name—my surname—was Young. That just happens to be a coincidence; it's a fairly common surname, after all, but Matthew sees it as a sign.

Then, when he put his back out playing golf and was in a lot of pain, Delia jokingly told him my cherry chocolate muffins always made her arthritis feel better. Matthew bought one and returned the next day insisting I'd done some kind of spell because all his pain had gone. I denied it, but he was right, and he somehow knew it, and he's now determined to prove I'm a witch.

I could stay here in the kitchen and let Delia and Cooper deal with him; neither of them like him, and they will happily evict him if the need arises. But I don't like letting other people fight my battles for me. I wipe my hands on a cloth and go out into the café.

"He was just leaving," Cooper says icily.

"I don't have my coffee yet," Matthew points out.

"It's all right, Cooper. Make his coffee. What can I do for you?" I ask Matthew calmly.

Matthew is tall, dark, and good looking, and he knows it. He's older than me, late thirties, and I believe he's panicking at the thought of turning forty. He's recently bought a sports car, he's out with a different girl every few weeks, and I'm guessing it's more difficult for him to stay in shape than it used to be five years ago, because he's always limping from sprained ankles. He's captain of the local football team and cricket team, but I'm convinced his tan is fake, and his teeth are far too white to be natural.

His shrewd brown eyes narrow, and his gaze slips down me, assessing my figure in my jeans and navy shirt. I bear his scrutiny with a lifted chin, refusing to give him the satisfaction of letting him know he's making me uncomfortable.

Even though he's never short of a date, and he's determined to prove I'm a witch, he frequently asks me out. I always decline as politely as I can, and he always looks surprised, as if he can't believe I've been able to resist his charms.

"You look good today," he says.

From the suit of armour over by the door, there's a slight squeak. Delia hears it and glances over, but Matthew doesn't react, so I'm guessing he thought it was someone's chair.

"What do you want?" I ask tiredly. "I'm busy."

"Detective Chief Inspector Hobbs said you witnessed the murder of Liza Banks," he says. "I wonder if you'd like to give me an account of last evening."

"No thank you."

"I'll pay you," he says.

For some reason, that comment brings heat to my cheeks. "I'm not talking to the press," I snap. "And I'm busy, so I'd like you to leave, please." I walk across the café to the door, open it, and turn to him pointedly.

He picks up his coffee, walks slowly over to me and stands in the doorway, then turns to face me.

"It's the spring equinox on Saturday," he says softly. "The pagan festival of Ostara. Will you be celebrating it?"

I stiffen. "I don't know what you're talking about."

He moves a little closer to me. "I don't believe you. I know you're a witch. Making all your muffins with magic. You'd have been hanged by now if you'd lived in the seventeenth century."

Unfortunately, he's probably right, and I have to still a shudder. "Please leave," I state clearly. "I'm busy."

He tips his head to study me, and his eyes take on a lewd glow. "Are you going to do a few spells, dance skyclad in the forest?" He's mocking me, and his use of the word skyclad, which means ritual nakedness, makes my face burn. "Can I watch?" he asks silkily.

There's another squeak from behind him. He hears this one and turns, right as the knight's arm swings forward with the sword. Matthew leaps out of the way with a yell, and the tip of the sword lands on the tiles with a clang.

He swears, loud and colourful, prompting a glare from one of the elderly customers sitting at a nearby table in the window.

"That nearly hit me!" he exclaims.

"Sorry about that," I tell him, not in the least bit truthfully.

"It's dangerous," he says. "I'm going to call the Council and get the Health and Safety Department to check it out."

"You do that." I gesture out of the door. "Goodbye."

His chest heaving, he pauses, and for a moment I think I'm going to have trouble getting him out. Out of the corner of my eye, I see Cooper twitch, and I have a vision of him leaping over the counter to come and rescue me. In the doorway, Merlin barks and then snarls, something he does very rarely.

Matthew obviously decides he's not going to win this time, and he walks out, avoiding Merlin, and strides off down the road.

I blow out a long breath and look at the suit of armour. I'm going to have to do something about that sword. I'll get some rope and tie it so his arm can't fall again.

I look up at the helm, and inhale sharply. The blue eyes are back. They stare unblinkingly into mine, the colour of a beautiful summer sky.

I stare at them, then move forward and lift the visor. It's empty.

"Shame it missed," Delia says, coming to stand beside me.

"Mm." My heart is hammering. I lower the visor and look down at the knight's arm. The sword lies across the doorway, blocking the entrance.

"Cooper," I call out, "can you bring me some rope from the break room?"

"Sure thing." He runs out, then reappears with a length of rope and comes over.

Together, we lift the knight's arm back into place, then loop the rope over it and secure it around his neck. Cooper ties it tightly. There's no chance now that the arm can fall.

I feel a twinge of regret. It's clear there is something unusual about the suit of armour, whether it's taken on its own life because it's so old, or if it's something else. I'd say it was cursed, but cursed objects don't rescue their owners! I'm convinced the sword falling was no accident, and he's saved me twice now. But I can't risk the sword falling on a customer.

"There." Cooper steps back. "That's one of my knots. He won't get free anytime soon."

"I think we need a cup of tea," Delia says, and we all nod, so she goes off to make a pot.

I walk to a nearby table and pick up some cups, then glance over at the knight. I can just see a glimmer of his blue eyes. He's watching me.

My lips curve up in a small smile, and I walk out to the kitchen.

Chapter Five

"How's your afternoon been?" Imogen asks. She's refused a coffee and the last lemon muffin, so I suspect she's here on business. Lemon aids weight loss, and with a spell that encourages a person to enjoy the benefits of a walk outdoors, these muffins are one treat people can eat without feeling guilty, and she usually loves them.

It's now five-thirty, and the light is fading, even though there's nearly an hour until sunset. The temperature has dropped since the storm, and there's a spring coolness to the air. Moths flutter around the café windows, making Merlin sneeze and snap at them in mid-air.

"Busy," I tell her. "Having all your police officers around has put us in overdrive."

"We do like our coffee and muffins," she admits.

She glances around the café. It's quieter now. Cooper's gone fishing with Duncan, and Delia is wiping down the tables. We close at six p.m., because by then the restaurants are opening, and everyone's looking for dinner rather than coffee and a snack.

"Can I steal Gwen for a while?" Imogen asks the older woman.

"Of course." Delia picks up some plates. "I'll stack the dishwasher."

"You can head out then," I tell her. "I'll close up. Thank you for your hard work today."

She smiles, and I tug on my coat and head out of the café, Merlin at my side.

"What can I do for you?" I ask Imogen.

"SOCO has cleared the library," Imogen explains. "We can go in now. I wonder whether you could walk me through what happened?"

I swallow hard at the thought of returning to the scene of the crime. But I say, "Of course."

"It won't take long," she promises. "I just want to make sure I have the events right in my mind."

"I understand."

It's a cool, clear evening. The sun is setting, turning the stones of Glastonbury Abbey to a warm amber. I grew up listening to my parents telling me stories about this place, and I learned to love both the history and the legend. Founded in the seventh century, the Abbey was destroyed by fire in 1184, then rebuilt, and eventually it became one of the richest monasteries in England. The myths that surround the area are even more rich and varied, linking it to the Isle of Avalon, and claiming connections to the Holy Grail and, of course, King Arthur, who is supposedly buried here with his queen, Guinevere.

Tonight, though, the stones bring me no comfort, as I think about the terrible event of the night before.

"How's Luke doing?" I ask Imogen.

"As you'd expect." She kicks at a stone with her toe. "Telling someone their wife has been murdered isn't one of the highlights of the job." Her voice is a little sharp.

I look across at her. Her dark brown hair is in her usual tight bun at the nape of her neck. As a detective chief inspector, she doesn't have to wear uniform, but she always dresses smartly, and today she's in a grey trouser suit with a crisp white shirt. She's a good soul, and my best friend. Although she didn't have the complication of dating Luke, she knew both he and Liza from school, so this must be upsetting for her, too.

"I'm sorry," I tell her softly. "I hope you don't think I was being gleeful."

"Gwen! Of course not." She frowns at me. "You're the nicest person in the universe. I'd never think that. It was awful, that's all. Luke cried when I told him. I've been angry with him for so long, for your sake, but right then all I felt was pity." She clears her throat. "I spoke to him this morning, and he said something really weird. He'd been to the library, to see where Liza died. And he said on the way out, he looked along the bookstacks, and he was convinced he saw her, just for a moment."

We exchange a glance. She doesn't want to ask whether I think Liza's haunting the library, but I know she's wondering if that's the case.

My throat tightens. I don't want to think about Liza being dead. About Luke having to go through with this. I'll never be able to forget what he did to me, but I have moved on. "Catch him, Immi. The murderer."

"I'll do my best." She smiles at me. "Can't you do a spell or something and tell me who did it?"

"Unfortunately, it doesn't work like that." I wish it did. People always think magic is done with a wave of a wand. The truth is that it's all about changing the natural forces around us with the power of intention, which takes a great deal of concentration and skill. I can affect people's emotions by using the food I bake to cast spells, but I can't tell the future or turn people into amphibians. More's the pity. Matthew Hopkins would make a great common toad.

"I know," Imogen says. "Come on, there's something odd I want to show you."

She opens the door to the library. I tell Merlin to stay put, then go into the cool foyer. She follows me in and closes the door.

Earlier, when I walked past, the place was full of SOCO in their white suits to ensure they didn't contaminate the murder scene. Now, it's mostly empty. A couple of officers stand at the end of the bookstacks, talking quietly, but it looks as if the reading room is empty.

"So talk me through it," Imogen says.

I explain how I walked through the stacks to the end and called Liza's name. "I thought I heard a sound from the reading room," I continue, "so I went in there."

We go through. My heart is banging hard on my ribs. The desks surrounding where Liza was found have been moved aside, and presumably SOCO have examined them thoroughly. In the centre of the room, tape on the tiles marks the place where Liza lay, like a scene out of a detective series.

We walk over to it, and I explain how I recognized her, then bent to check her pulse. "I couldn't find it," I say, my voice husky. "I realized she was dead."

"Okay." Imogen's voice is calm. "What happened then?"

"I thought the murderer was probably still in the room, so I turned and fled back down the corridor and out through the main doors. I heard footsteps behind me, so I knew they were chasing me."

Imogen nods. "Anything else?"

"No, I don't think so."

"You didn't stop to pick anything up, move anything?"

"No. I went straight out."

"Okay." She nods and walks behind the taped figure on the floor and studies the tiles thoughtfully, then glances over her shoulder. "Come and look at this."

I follow her and look down at the tiles. There's a fine powder on the floor, like dust except it has a greenish tinge like powdered herbs, and in it someone has drawn a line, about twelve inches wide. Underneath that is another line with a semi-circle halfway along.

"What do you reckon?" she asks.

I frown. "Could it have been caused by someone moving a desk."

"Maybe. But to me it looks more like it's been drawn with a finger. It's neat and regular."

I nod. She's right. I study it for a moment. Something is poking at my memory. I've seen it before, but not quite like this…

"Come with me," she says. She walks a few feet to the right, then drops to her haunches and points to more marks.

"Another symbol?" I bend to examine it. This one looks like the letter W, but with rounded ends, not pointed.

She stands, then continues around the room, pointing out another ten symbols. The next is an arrow. Then a V with a loop. Then two zig-zag lines, one on top of the other.

And then I realize what they are. "Come with me," I tell her.

I go over to the stairs and up to the mezzanine floor that runs around the edge of the circular room. It's several feet wide, enough for two people to pass. Bookshelves line the outer wall. On the other side of the walkway is a waist-high barrier. I lean on it and look down at the scene, and Imogen joins me. The symbols are just about visible, in a loose circle, around the place where Liza fell. Up here, it's much clearer what they are.

"They're the glyphs for the twelve astrological signs," I tell her. I point them out, starting with the V that ends in a loop. "That's Capricorn." I point to the two zigzag lines. "That's Aquarius." Then the two semi-circles back to back with a line through the middle. "Pisces." I continue around the room, pointing out each star sign in turn.

"Wow," Imogen says in awe. "I'd never have guessed that." She frowns. "What do they mean?"

"I've no idea."

"Is it something witchy?"

"I really don't know," I admit. "Astrology does play a part in witchcraft sometimes. But I don't know what this means."

"Well, thank you anyway, for deducing what the glyphs are. Even if I'm not sure why they're here, I still know more than I did this morning."

"How did Liza die?" I ask Imogen as we walk downstairs, realizing I don't know.

"She was strangled with fishing line."

I stop walking and press my fingers to my lips.

"Sorry," Imogen says, "you did ask."

"I did." I suspected she'd been strangled, but the fishing line surprises me, for some reason.

Astrology and fishing… Briefly, I remember Cooper reading out my horoscope earlier. Not long ago, he headed off to go fishing with his dad. But I can't believe it was he who murdered Liza. Cooper's a sweetheart, fun and genuine, a lovely young man, and the thought of him murdering someone is laughable. I refuse to start suspecting everyone around me.

"Do you think whoever did it will kill again?" I ask her. "Or was it likely to have been a one-off, a crime of passion?"

She tips her head from side to side. "Liza wasn't hit over the head with the first object at hand. I think the killer went there with the fishing line to kill her. It was cold and calculating. But was it the action of a serial killer who's going to kill again?" She blows out a long breath. "I don't think so. Don't quote me on that, though."

I carry on walking down the stairs. "Are you going home now?" I ask her.

"No, I'll be heading back to the station to file a report and begin the investigation. I'm just going to take a stroll through the offices." Her tone is nonchalant, but I know her better than that.

"Checking out if there's a tall, dark, and sexy exhibition officer working late?" I tease. She's had her eye on Christian Wheeler since he started work at the museum earlier this year. She swears she's not interested, but I've seen the way her gaze lingers on him when he comes into the café.

"Not at all, and I'll thank you not to cast aspersions on my professional behaviour."

I laugh. "I saw him earlier. I think he's in his office. I'll leave you to go and find out."

"No!" She looks alarmed. "Come with me."

"What are we, fourteen?"

"He makes me nervous."

I chuckle. "I didn't think anyone made you nervous." Usually she's so calm and in control. It's strange to see her go to pieces over a guy.

She scowls at me, but heads across the reading room floor to the museum offices on the other side, and I follow her, smiling.

Chapter Six

Sure enough, Christian Wheeler is in his office. Imogen stops in the doorway, and as I watch her observe him, I know she's unaware of the way her expression softens and a slight flush appears on her cheeks. He has his back to us, studying a large pinboard on which he's pinned various pictures of artefacts, printed articles, and handwritten notes. Christian helps a lot at the Arthurian Adventure, but his main job is planning the exhibitions in the museum.

Imogen swallows, opens her mouth to say something, then shakes her head and backs toward the door. But I'm not going to let her get away with that. I clear my throat loudly, and Christian turns.

"Oh," he says, his eyebrows rising. "Sorry, I didn't hear you come in. Hi, Gwen."

"Hey, Christian."

His gaze moves to Imogen. "Detective Chief Inspector."

"Dr. Wheeler," Imogen says. Christian has a PhD, so the title is correct, but it's a bit formal. She's terrible at flirting, but then she is technically on duty, so I suppose I should give her a little leeway.

"Are you working on a new exhibition?" I ask, hoping to cover for her.

"Yes," he replies, "on the Tudor period."

"Oh, that'll be great." Glastonbury Abbey has such a fascinating history. During the Dissolution of the Monasteries, the abbey was suppressed. Its treasures were seized, the monks dispersed, and the last abbot, who refused to submit to King Henry, was hanged, drawn, and quartered. It's a fascinating part of history, and although my first love has always been the Dark Ages—the period when the Romans left Britain, the time of Arthur—I'm also interested in many other parts of English history.

I'm excited about the exhibition, but Imogen doesn't say anything, and I hold in my enthusiasm. She studies Christian thoughtfully. He studies her back.

"What can I do for you?" Christian asks.

I can see why he makes Imogen flustered. He's a smart guy, rather serious, and he doesn't suffer fools gladly. He has a habit of looking over his scholarly, dark-rimmed glasses at you as he waits for you to answer a question, and if I didn't know him better, I think I'd get flustered too. But I'm always in the museum and the library so I get to speak to him a lot, and I've learned that his sense of humour is dry rather than non-existent, and that he has a kind heart. He was very good to me when Mum died, and he helped me with the paperwork for the shop, for which I'll be ever thankful.

"I'm just making a final sweep of the premises," Imogen says. "Making sure nobody's thought of anything else that might be helpful."

He perches on the edge of the desk. "I've been thinking about it all day, but nothing's come to mind." He shakes his head. "I still can't believe it happened while I was in my office. If only I'd heard something, or decided to leave a bit earlier…" He runs a hand through his hair. He would have worked closely with Liza, so it's not surprising he's upset.

"You weren't to know," Imogen says softly. "You can't blame yourself. None of us can. All we can do is try our best to find out who did it."

"Yes," he says. "And I've heard you're the best officer to get to the bottom of things."

She doesn't know what to say to that, and just stares down at her boots. Christian's lips curve up. He likes her. I wasn't sure before, but as he looks at her now, his eyes are warm. His gaze slides to me, and I can see he's amused at how flustered she is.

She lifts her gaze and studies him for a long moment. Then she says, "Do you go fishing, Christian?"

He tips his head to the side. "What's this about? Am I a suspect?"

She opens her mouth to reply, but at that moment footsteps sound behind me, and a female voice says, "Oh, I'm so sorry. I didn't realize you were busy."

Mary Paxton owns the local florist. Although she's only in her late thirties, she doesn't dye her hair, and draws her salt-and-pepper locks back in a loose ponytail. She's wrapped up against the cool spring breeze in a smart black coat and woollen gloves. She's also carrying a bouquet of beautiful spring flowers, tied with a large pink bow.

"That's okay." Christian stands to take the bouquet from her. "Thanks so much for delivering this. I would've come in to pick it up."

"It's no problem," Mary says. "I was passing." She gives me and Imogen a small smile. "Good evening."

"Hello, Mary," we both say.

I don't know her well, but about six months ago, just before my mother died, I had an interesting conversation with her that led to us having a closer connection. She came into the café, ordered a latte, and took a seat at a table in the corner. While Cooper was preparing her drink, she started dabbing her eyes with a tissue, clearly upset. When I took her coffee over, I noticed a library book sticking out of the bag by her feet. Its title was Understanding Cancer. I sat opposite her and asked her gently whether she wanted to talk about it, and after looking shocked that I'd noticed, she finally started talking. She told me her mother had been diagnosed with breast cancer. At that stage, my mum was also very ill, so the two of us were able to talk about the difficulties of caring for a sick parent, brought together by our emotional hardship. My mum died just a few weeks later, and Mary came to the funeral and gave me a lovely hug and helped at the wake, handing out food and washing up afterward.

There's an awkward silence. Christian is looking at Imogen, frowning. Her cheeks have flushed. I think she's embarrassed by the questions she felt she had to ask, and she's also shaken by the flowers he's had delivered. It's obvious what conclusion she's drawn from them.

She clears her throat. "Well, thank you, Dr. Wheeler. Please let me know if any details come to mind." She turns and walks from the office.

Christian looks at me and gives a long, disappointed sigh. I shoot him a smile, say goodbye to Mary, and head out.

"You're wrong," I tell Imogen when I catch up with her in the reading room.

"About what?"

"I'm sure those flowers weren't for a woman," I tell her. "Or at least, not for a love interest."

"I don't know what you're talking about." She opens the library door and walks out briskly.

I sigh and catch the door, then exclaim as Merlin slips through and runs past me. "Here, boy," I call, turning to follow him. To my surprise, he stops in the middle of the bookstacks and stares.

A person is standing in the shadows. I open my mouth to say something, but the words refuse to come as I realize who it is.

Liza.

A heartbeat later, she vanishes.

Merlin barks, then huffs a big sigh, as if he's exasperated.

My heart bangs against my ribs, and my chest heaves with rapid breaths. I blink rapidly to clear my vision, half-expecting her to reappear, but she doesn't. The bookstacks remain quiet, motes of dust dancing in the shaft of late sunlight coming through the high window.

"Hey." Imogen's voice behind me makes me jump. "You coming?"

"Yes, yes."

"Are you all right?" She frowns. "You look like you've seen a..."

"I did."

"What?"

"I saw Liza. Standing just there." I point.

Imogen stares. "So Luke was right—he definitely saw her."

"Looks that way. The weird thing? I think Merlin saw her, too."

"That is pretty weird."

"Only I could have a psychic dog."

We both study the area, half waiting for her to reappear, but it remains empty, quiet and cool. Merlin trots past us and goes out the door that Imogen's holding. We exchange a glance, turn, and follow him out.

"Why is she still here?" Imogen asks. "Why hasn't she... you know... passed on to wherever you go when you die?"

"I don't know." I feel edgy and upset. I clear my throat. "About Christian..."

"I'd rather not talk about it," she says.

So we walk in silence, Merlin trotting quietly at my heels until we reach the café.

"I'll see you tomorrow," I tell Imogen. I feel tired and overwhelmed emotionally. I just want to be alone with my thoughts.

She stops and turns to me with a pained expression. "I'm sorry, Gwen. It's just, well, I've got a lot on my mind, and I can't let myself be distracted by all this nonsense."

"I know." She's running a murder enquiry. She had to ask Christian those questions, even though she really likes him, knowing it was going to annoy him. What a terrible position to be in.

She comes over to me and hugs me. "I'll see you tomorrow, okay? Get a good night's sleep."

"You, too," I tell her.

"Are you closing up now?"

"Yeah. I'll just sweep the floor and wipe the counter."

"You want me to stay? I don't like leaving you alone."

"I'll be fine," I say. "You said you didn't think we had a serial killer on our hands."

"Maybe, but I'm not taking any chances."

"Even so." I smile and ruffle Merlin's ear. "Merlin will take care of me."

"Of course he will, you sweet boy." She drops to her haunches in front of him and kisses the top of his head, and he licks her face. "You little darling. You look after Gwen, okay?"

She straightens and gives me a last smile. "See you tomorrow."

"Yes, see you."

Delia's locked the café, so I unlock it and let myself in, then lock it again behind me. I wave to Imogen as she gets in her car, and watch it drive away.

Phew, what a long day. But I still need to go through my routine. I put on the radio, get my broom, brush the floor, then wipe down the counter. My head's buzzing, and I feel a little jumpy, but I put that down to what happened in the library earlier. I wish I knew more about the astrological signs or why her ghost is haunting the library, but my magical skills are limited. I bake cookies that make people happy. It's not rocket science.

I lean the broom against the wall and switch off the light. The café is in semi-darkness, lit only from the light that's on in the break room behind me. I turn to give one last look around.

And then I stop and inhale sharply. The blue eyes are back behind the visor.

I freeze, staring at the suit of armour from across the room. The light from behind me is shining directly on the knight. I'm not mistaken. There's definitely someone inside the suit.

I wait, my heart pumping furiously, to see if the eyes vanish. This time, though, they don't.

After about thirty seconds, I walk around the counter and stand with my back to it, facing the knight. The eyes are still there, watching me. He doesn't move, though.

I wait another thirty seconds, then walk slowly up to him.

With a shaking hand, I lift the visor. Then I gasp. The eyes haven't disappeared. They're still there, bright blue, looking straight into mine.

I back up until I bump into the table behind me. "Who are you?" I demand. "What are you doing inside the suit?"

"I'm a friend," he says. It's the first time he's spoken. His voice is deep and gravelly and makes a shiver run down my spine. "Don't be alarmed," he adds.

"Don't be…" I give a short hysterical laugh. He blinks, and the corners of his eyes crinkle a little as if he's smiling. I glance down at Merlin, wondering why he's not barking his head off. He's sitting in front of the knight, looking up at him with… dare I say it… adoration?

"Can you help me get the helmet off?" The knight moves his arm a little, the one I tied up with rope. It squeaks. "I appear to be restrained."

"You nearly cut someone's head off," I point out. "Twice." My heart's racing so fast I think I'm going to pass out.

"They both deserved it." He squeaks again. "Please? I want to talk to you."

"You can talk with the helmet on." I don't want to go near him.

"It's hot in here," he points out.

I don't know what to say to that. He doesn't sound like a madman. He sounds calm and lucid. I think it's me who's going round the bend.

"Please," he says again. "I just want to talk."

I shake my head. "Not until you tell me who you are."

"All right." His eyes bore into mine. "I'm Arthur."

Chapter Seven

I pull out a chair and sit down hurriedly.

"Arthur?" I repeat.

"Yes." He moves his head inside the helm. "Can you help me take it off now?"

"Arthur who?" I ask him.

"You know me as Arthur Pendragon," he says.

I stare at him. "*The* Arthur?"

"The one and only." The corners of his eyes crinkle again.

"King Arthur?" I clarify. "The one with the round table and Excalibur?"

He shifts, the suit of armour squeaking around him. "I was never a king. I was a warrior. It was a long time ago, and things get twisted over the centuries."

"I don't understand."

"I'll explain everything," he promises. "Only, please, can you help me take this helm off?"

His eyes are pleading. Cautiously, I get to my feet. What a load of rubbish. He's obviously not who he claims—this is some elaborate prank. Resentment flares inside me and makes me lift my chin and glare at him. As if I don't have enough to cope with this week!

"I'll take off the helm," I tell him, "but then I want you to explain yourself."

"Okay." His blue eyes watch me as I approach him, and they continue watching as I hold the helm, undo the clip that someone in the museum must have put there to make sure it couldn't fall off, and then carefully lift it off his head.

I place it on the table and step back. He doesn't ask me to untie his hand, and I don't offer.

He smiles. "Hello."

He has black hair with flecks of grey at the temples, and he's clean shaven. He has strong features and doesn't look unlike the bust I've seen in the museum of the Roman emperor, Julius Caesar. I think he's in his mid-thirties.

He's gorgeous.

I try not to notice. "All right," I tell him. I feel a little calmer now I can see he's a real person. "Time for you to explain."

"It's difficult to know where to start," he says.

"How about you begin with why you're inside the suit of armour in my café?"

He surveys me thoughtfully. I can see he's thinking about what to say. "It's complicated," he says eventually.

"All right. I'll make it easier for you. How long have you been in there?"

"Inside the suit?" He thinks about it. "About four hundred and eighty."

"Seconds? Minutes?"

"Years."

I stare at him. That would mean he's been inside it since about the time of the English Reformation, when Glastonbury Abbey was suppressed. "What?"

"Well, not technically inside it."

"You've lost me."

"I don't quite understand it myself." A frown flickers on his brow. "My memory is a bit… fuzzy." He looks away, out of the window into the dark night.

I study his face, with his straight nose, strong jaw, and firm lips. A tingle runs down my spine. But I can't let myself be taken in by him just because he's handsome.

"What's your real name?" I ask.

His blue eyes come back to me. "I told you, it's Arthur."

I grit my teeth. "Okay, Arthur. You need to come clean with me, right now, or I'm going to call the police."

"You can call Imogen if you like," he says. "I don't mind. I rather like her."

My back stiffens. "How do you know about her? Have you been watching us?"

I expect him to deny it, but he says, "Of course. I've been watching you since you were born." He smiles.

I don't know what to think, what to feel. Coming from any other man, his words would puzzle me, maybe even scare me, but his eyes are so gentle, so full of tender affection that it makes me almost tearful. "I don't understand," I tell him, fighting against panic.

"I'll try to explain," he says. "About one thousand five hundred years ago, I fought in a battle in which I was mortally wounded."

"Camlann," I whisper, forgetting that I don't believe him. It was supposed to be Arthur's final battle against the invading Saxons.

He nods. "I was dying. I remember being on the battlefield, surrounded by the bodies of fallen warriors, in terrible pain." His brow furrows. "Some of my men took me by boat through the marshes to the nearby Isle of Avalon, where my sister lived. She was the high priestess of a coven of witches."

My jaw drops. "You mean Morgana."

"Yes. They brought my wife there to be with me. I remember lying in her arms, looking up at her."

He's talking about Guinevere. Unbidden, my eyes fill with tears. He notices them, and just smiles.

"Morgana told me she wouldn't let me die," he says. "And then she cast a spell…" His gaze slides to the pommel of his sword. "Do you see the metal plate on the pommel?"

"Yes."

"Unscrew it."

I stare at him for a moment. The pommel unscrews? I lift a hand and take it in my fingers. Then I try to turn it anticlockwise. It doesn't move.

"It's not been undone for hundreds of years," Arthur says, "it's a bit stiff. Like me."

Giving him a wry look, I turn it with more force and then, to my surprise, the top gives and turns in my fingers. It's like a lid. I unscrew it fully and take it off to reveal the inside of the pommel. It contains a small red gem, about half an inch long, held there by metal claws.

"It looks like a ruby," I say in awe. "She created a soulstone."

He studies the way it catches the light. "They originally placed it in the church altar. The Abbey grew up around that old church."

I'm astounded. "You were there at the foundation of the Abbey?"

His gaze is still fixed on the ruby. "Time meant nothing to me. Years passed, then decades, then centuries. People came to see the place where the mythical King Arthur was supposed to be buried with his queen. And then they came to destroy the Abbey."

"The Reformation," I whisper.

"The monks were afraid the king's men would take the ruby. So they placed it in this sword, with an old suit of armour. The men didn't look twice at it. I stood at the back of the Abbey for years, until one day they took me to the museum. And then eventually, I came back to you." His gaze returns to me.

"Back to me?" I'm confused.

"To my wife." His eyes are very blue. "Guinevere."

There's a long, long silence.

"I'm not Guinevere," I say eventually.

"It's your name."

"My name's Gwen."

"It may be a modern translation, but it still has the same origins."

"I'm not your wife," I tell him gently. "She died a long time ago."

"I know. I've been waiting for her to be reborn."

My heart bangs against my ribs. "You're talking about reincarnation."

He nods.

I feel a little faint. "You're saying I'm a reincarnation of Guinevere. The one from the legends."

"No, the real Guinevere. The wife I adored, and who adored me." His gaze is firm, brooking no argument. For a moment, I completely believe he was the infamous warrior who held back the invading Saxons for years.

I blink. "That's crazy!"

"A little, I suppose."

"A little!" I'm shaking. "How do you know I'm her?"

"You look just like her." He smiles. "Beautiful as ever."

"Stop it!" I'm close to tears now. "You appear in my café, inside the suit of armour that's stood here for years, and you tell me you're King Arthur and I'm the reincarnation of your dead wife, and I'm supposed to just believe you?"

"I'm not a king." He doesn't look alarmed or frustrated. He just says, "But the rest of it is the truth."

"Even if that is the case, what do you expect is going to happen? Do you think I'm just going to fall into your arms? Declare my undying love for you? Because if so, you're dreaming."

His smile fades, and he looks at the floor. The look of disappointment on his face makes me want to cry.

"I can't listen to this." I desperately need to get away, to gather my wits.

"You want me to go?" he asks.

I speak without hesitation. "Yes."

"All right. If you want me to come back, just ask."

I walk toward the counter, then stop and turn. "And what if—" I stop.

With a racing heart, I stare at the suit of armour. The helm is still sitting on the table, but Arthur is no longer inside the suit.

He's gone.

I wait for about twenty seconds, then walk up to it. Cautiously, I peer inside it. It's empty.

My gaze slides to the ruby in the pommel of the sword. It catches the light and glints, almost as if he's winking at me.

Slowly, I screw the lid of the pommel back, then lift the helm, place it on the suit, and clip it into place. Merlin is still sitting in front of it, but he stands now and whines a little.

"Come on," I say softly, and he trots after me as I walk behind the counter, collect my coat, and then head out of the back door.

*

For the second time that week, I call in at Beatrix's house on the way home.

"Hello," she says when she opens the door. "Oh no, don't tell me there's been another murder."

"No, nothing like that." I go inside, follow Merlin through to the living room, and hug Max. "But something strange happened tonight."

"I'll make tea," Max says, "and then you can tell us all about it."

So, over a cup of tea and a chocolate Hobnob, I go through the events of the evening—from discovering the astrological signs in the library, to what happened with the suit of armour.

They both sit and stare at me, their biscuits halfway to their mouths, their jaws dropping in amazement, as I relay my story. When I'm done, I sit there sipping my tea, rather enjoying their stunned expressions, as it doesn't make me feel quite so foolish.

"Arthur…" Beatrix murmurs. "Well, it's plausible…"

I laugh. "Seriously?"

"Of course," she says. "We know that Glastonbury was an island as far back as the Iron Age. You told me there was archaeological evidence for it."

"Yes, but—"

"And we know that it was almost certainly the Isle of Avalon mentioned in the legends."

"Yes, I get that, but—"

"It's Arthur's resting place," she says. "It contains the tombs of both Arthur and Guinevere."

"I can see what you're saying, although—"

"You're a witch," Beatrix states. "You do magic. Why is it so unbelievable that the soul of this ancient warrior has been captured in a soulstone?"

"Arthur," I state. "King Arthur."

"You said he vanished from the suit of armour. Just dematerialized. And now you're trying to convince me he's not magical in some way?"

"I'm trying to convince myself." I look down at Merlin. "He just sat in front of the knight and looked up at him adoringly."

"Dogs have a sixth sense," Max states. "I read that once."

I look at my uncle, whose kind face is creased in a frown that shows he's trying to understand. "Do you think it's possible?" I ask him.

"I didn't use to believe in witches. And then I met Beatrix, who can change things with the wave of a brush." He shrugs. "I'm willing to hear him out."

"But…" I look down into my teacup. "He said I was the wife he adored, and who adored him. Does he expect me just to fall into his arms and marry him all over again?"

"Was he hot?" Beatrix asks.

"What? I…" My face burns with the heat of a thousand suns.

She tries not to laugh, and I scowl at her, then my lips curve up, and then we're all laughing. "He was gorgeous," I admit. "Very handsome. But does that mean I should just throw all caution to the wind?"

"Of course not. We know nothing about him," Beatrix says. "Well, almost nothing. But if he's a good man, a decent man, he'll give you time to get to know him, and he won't presume you're his, just because he says so."

"Guinevere," Max murmurs, tipping his head to the side as he surveys me. "It makes a lot of sense."

"Because my name's Gwen?" I try to make my voice sharp, but I'm not great at sarcasm, and it comes out kind of hopeful.

"It's an odd coincidence," Max says, "but that's not the only thing. You've always been fascinated with Arthur, even since you were a little girl."

"That's true," Beatrix adds. "You had that storybook about him that you used to make me read to you over and over again."

"I don't remember that." It's a lie. I still have it, and I still get it out and read it every now and again. *The Tales of King Arthur*. It reminds me of my mum, and of my childhood. It's dog-eared and a little tatty now, but the hand-drawn pictures of Arthur and Guinevere are beautiful.

In them, she has red hair, like me. But it's just a coincidence.

"He's the reason you wanted to become an archaeologist," she reminds me. "You've always had a fascination with Glastonbury."

"That's because I live there."

She fixes me with a steady gaze. "I can see how much this has thrown you, and it's good that you're wary. Scepticism is healthy. Just make sure you don't miss out on a wonderful opportunity because you've failed to keep an open mind. If he's telling the truth, and he is Arthur, and you were once his Guinevere, he's been waiting for you for nearly fifteen hundred years. I'd say that makes him a pretty devoted husband."

"I…" Words fail me. "But… even if that was the case, there would hardly be a happy ending. He's imprisoned in a suit of armour. I can't imagine it leading to a normal life for either of us."

"He's imprisoned in the ruby," she reminds me, "not the suit. I wonder what would happen if you took it out of the sword and had it made into a necklace or something else he could wear?"

My jaw drops. "You really think that would work?"

"I don't see why not. The ruby is the key to his presence here. Free the ruby, and I'm convinced you'll be able to free the man."

Chapter Eight

"Are you okay?" Cooper frowns at me as I go to deliver his beautiful flat whites with the carefully drawn leaf in the foamed milk to the customer. "That's the third time you've spilled coffee this morning," he scolds.

It's the next day, and I'm in the café in body, but not in mind, which is somewhere else completely.

"I'm all fingers and thumbs today." I smile to cover the fact that my hands are shaking.

"Let me do that," he says, taking the two coffee cups from me, and he proceeds to take them over to the table by the window. Sighing, I join Delia behind the glass and begin making a fresh batch of muffin mixture.

"He only wants to chat up the girl with the ponytail." Delia grins and gestures to the brunette that Cooper's now talking to.

"Aw," I say, "in that case I'm happy to help."

She gives me a curious look. "Are you okay, though? Cooper's right, you do seem a bit jittery."

"I'm fine. Just didn't get much sleep, that's all." I refuse to look across at the suit of armour. When I got in this morning, Delia was already there, and the suit of armour was empty. I'm guessing Arthur won't reappear until we're alone again tonight. There are no blue eyes behind the visor, and yet I'm sure I can still feel him watching me as I bake and stack the cabinet and carry coffees to customers. *I've been watching you since you were born.* The words make me shiver.

But there's nothing I can do about it, so I try to put him out of my mind.

It's impossible, of course. He's all I can think about. He's the reason why I struggled to sleep last night. He and Beatrix. I thought when I told her about him that she'd be annoyed at his presumptuousness and tell me to stay far away from him. And instead…

If he's telling the truth, and he is Arthur, and you were once his Guinevere, he's been waiting for you for nearly fifteen hundred years. I'd say that makes him a pretty devoted husband.

It can't be true. It just can't. It's ridiculous. A fantasy fairy tale I want to believe because it's incredible and romantic, and it would be lovely to think I'm somehow special. I love my life here, but I'm lonely, and I haven't even dated anyone since Luke because Mum was ill for so long, so it would be amazing to know the man I've been destined to be with has been waiting for me all this time.

But then I get a swell of panic and feel as if I want to open the door and run out and just keep on running. The way he looked at me... as if he knew me intimately... *The wife I adored and who adored me...*

"Gwen!" Delia reaches out and stops my hand. I look down and realize I was about to pour chocolate chips into my cheese and bacon muffins.

"Eek." I put the bowl aside hastily. "I like chocolate, but that's ridiculous."

"Why don't you go for a walk?" she asks helpfully, trying not to look at Allison and Joss, who are laughing behind us. "Clear your mind? It's quiet at the moment. Plenty of time to get ready for lunch."

"Yes, all right." I give them a wry look. "And you two can stop sniggering."

"We're just unused to you being so distracted," Joss, the young cheeky one, says. "Don't tell me... you have a man on your mind."

My face fills with heat, and they all grin with delight. "Who's the lucky guy?" Allison asks.

"He's not... I mean... No one." I blush even more. "Okay, I'm outta here."

Leaving their laughter behind, I grab my coat, call Merlin, and head out of the back door so I don't have to walk past the knight.

It's a cool, fresh spring day. Tulips, hyacinths, and peonies fill the gardens of the houses I pass. Normally I love this time of year, but I don't feel as if I can appreciate its beauty at the moment.

I walk around the building and cross the car park toward the Abbey. There's an entrance fee to the grounds, but I have a year pass because I go in so often. Oscar, the guy on the gate, lets me through with a smile. I walk through the Lady Chapel and out the other end. This was once the nave of the main church, but it's now open to the air, the floor covered with grass. The blue sky reminds me of Arthur's eyes.

I'm going to have to talk to him tonight. I should have asked him more questions last night, but I'm not going to be harsh on myself for panicking and needing to get away. Today, even though I feel anxious about the outcome, my head is clear. Beatrix has put my mind at rest, and I don't feel as frightened of him. I have lots of questions to ask. And she's right, if he's a good person, if he truly is the knight the legends speak of, he will understand and be patient with me.

Free the ruby, and I'm convinced you'll be able to free the man. Is Beatrix right? Is it truly possible to release Arthur from the suit? What will happen then—will he be able to leave the café and go out into the world like a normal person? And if he is able, will he want to leave Glastonbury?

The suit of armour could stay in the café where it always has. Nothing would change.

So why do I feel such a sharp sense of loss at the thought of Arthur leaving?

I stop walking. Without meaning to, my feet have led me up the nave to the site of King Arthur's tomb. It's a rectangular grave, facing east-west the way all graves do in Christian churchyards. The plaque reads:

"Site of King Arthur's Tomb. In the year 1191 the bodies of King Arthur and his queen were said to have been found on the south side of the Lady Chapel. On 19th April 1278 their remains were removed in the presence of King Edward I and Queen Eleanor to a black marble tomb on this site. This tomb survived until the Dissolution of the Abbey in 1539."

It's said that medieval monks invented the discovery of the bodies to encourage more visitors to the abbey after it was burned down in 1184. That would certainly make sense, especially as the legendary Arthur was growing in popularity at that time, due to two writers, Geoffrey of Monmouth and Chrétien de Troyes. Between them, they turned the Romano-British leader into a romantic medieval-style king, inventing the legends of Excalibur, Merlin, the Knights of the Round Table, and the Holy Grail. No doubt followers of the stories would have travelled from far and wide to see the graves of the famous king and queen.

The evidence for the 'real' Arthur is shady, buried beneath layers of myth and legend, in the aptly named Dark Ages. If he did exist, he was almost certainly a warrior who fought against the invading Anglo-

Saxons in the late fifth to early sixth centuries. The man in the suit of armour told me himself, "I was never a king. I was a warrior. It was a long time ago, and things get twisted over the centuries."

But what if he did exist, and if he is buried here? With his queen?

A cold shiver like an icy finger trails down my spine. I do believe in reincarnation, and like many people, I've often experienced déjà vu, and felt as if I've been to places and done things before. But could it really be possible that I was once married to the legendary Arthur of Britain?

I close my eyes and feel the spring breeze blowing across my face. I think about my mother, and how we used to sit curled up on the sofa, reading *The Tales of King Arthur*. At that point, I knew nothing about the real Arthur, only the legend of him as king with his knights and Merlin and the sword in the stone. I remember looking with Mum at the drawing of Arthur and Guinevere's wedding. They were in the throne room in Camelot, and she was dressed in a glittering golden gown, with a gold crown on her red hair. Arthur was dressed in a richly embroidered blue tunic and wore a crown, and he stared lovingly into her eyes.

Of course, there are also all the stories about her falling in love with Lancelot, tales I disliked immensely, as I hated the thought of her being unfaithful. I wanted her to be in love with Arthur, and I wanted the two of them to be happy. I've never really thought about the intensity with which I wished this, but if I were her, it would all make sense…

I open my eyes and turn away from the grave. I can't let myself get caught up in fanciful dreams. That's not reality. Real life is Liza, strangled with fishing line, and the murderer who's still on the loose. Not knights in shining armour, and gold crowns…

I exit the grounds in a dream, then blink, startled, as someone calls, "Gwen!" Turning, I gasp as I see who it is.

"Luke," I whisper.

He walks up to me, his hands in the pockets of his jeans, his shoulders hunched. His face is pale, his hair unruly.

"Hey," he says.

"Luke…" Without thinking, I move close and put my arms around him.

He holds me tightly for a long time. Then he finally releases me. There are tears on both our cheeks when we part.

"I'm so, so sorry," I say softly.

"Thank you." He wipes his face, then runs his hand through his hair. "Imogen said you were the last person to talk to Liza."

I nod. "She came into the café before she went to the library. She bought a cake to celebrate getting the promotion at the field unit."

"She told you, then." He gives a short, humourless laugh.

I resist the urge to say, *Of course she did.* "She was very excited about it," I say instead. "It's such a terrible shame."

He looks away, over at the Abbey. He's a handsome man, but his features look ravaged with grief. He won't be the same after this. "How could anyone do that?" His voice is hoarse. "She was so beautiful, so full of life... I loved her so much..."

Even after all this time, I feel a little twist inside me at his words. I loved him once, and it still hurts to think about him loving someone else. But I feel no pleasure at the thought that he's lost Liza. Nobody deserves to lose their partner in such a way.

Briefly, I think of Guinevere being at Arthur's side when he died, and the knight's words, *I remember lying in her arms, looking up at her.* I push the thought away.

"I saw her," Luke says. "I had to identify the body."

I frown in sympathy. "Oh, how awful."

He swallows hard. "It was so odd. It was as if it wasn't her. Do you think she's in heaven now?"

A couple of thoughts whip through my mind—the rather wicked thought that she wasn't a very nice person, so she might not have made it that far, as well as the memory of seeing her ghost, which means she's almost certainly bound to this plane. But I don't say either of those. Instead, I say, "I'm sure she is, Luke."

He rubs his nose. "Her pendant was missing," he says distractedly.

"What do you mean? What pendant?"

"The one she always wore. It was a Tudor rose. Her mother gave it to her. She never took it off. I don't know where it went. Imogen thinks the murderer might have removed it."

My gaze slides across to the library building as something flickers in my mind. Christian, who's working on a Tudor exhibition, and clearly has a love of the period. Surely not...

"I'd better go," Luke says. "I'm going to the funeral home, to make arrangements."

"I wish I could say something to make it better," I tell him.

He meets my eyes. "Tell me who did it," he says. "That's the only thing that would make me feel better at the moment."

I open my mouth, but no words come out. "I'm sorry," I whisper.

He sighs and studies his shoes. "I know. I've just got to wait and see whether the police can work it out." He gives me a brief smile. "See you later."

"See you. Take care of yourself."

He doesn't reply to that, just walks away, his shoulders hunched against the breeze. My eyes fill with tears, but there's nothing I can say to ease his pain, so I remain silent.

I turn and look across at the café. The knight by the door is clearly visible.

Suddenly, more than anything, I wish it was late and the café was closed, and I could talk to him.

I cross the car park and go into the café, pause in front of him, and look up at the visor.

His blue eyes look into mine. "I'm sorry," he whispers.

I stare into them for a long time. Then I turn and walk across to the kitchen, and carry on making the cheese and bacon muffins.

Chapter Nine

Imogen calls in mid-afternoon to pick up a latte.

"How's the investigation going?" I ask.

She blows out a breath and leans on the counter. "I'm supposed to say we're making significant progress."

"Are you?"

"Nope. Not really."

"Do you have any suspects?" Cooper asks.

"I can't really go into specifics," she apologizes. She glances at me, and I know she's thinking about Christian. Has she had to interrogate him any further? I think about what Luke told me about the Tudor Rose pendant and shift awkwardly.

"By the way," she asks Cooper, "I'm sorry to have to ask, but where were you on the evening of the seventeenth?"

"Me?" Cooper stares at her. "Am I a suspect, then?"

"It's important to rule everyone out."

"Okay…" His gaze slides to me, then back to her. "I went fishing with my dad. Gwen saw me go."

Imogen looks at me, and I nod. "Just before five o'clock," I tell her.

"You went straight to him at the field unit?" she asks.

"I met him out by the car." His brow creases. "I hope you don't think I did it. I mean, I didn't like Liza that much, she wasn't very nice to Gwen, but I didn't hate her. I'd never kill anyone."

Imogen's expression softens. "I know. It's important that I have the full picture, that's all. That I know who was where. You didn't see anyone coming in or out of the building at that time?"

"Patience and Bernard came out together." Patience is the head librarian, and Bernard works with her. "And Christian," he adds. "He came running out to his car. He waved and said he'd left something in there."

Christian told us he was in his office from five until six p.m. He didn't mention leaving at all. I look at Imogen. She doesn't look at me.

"Anything else?" she asks.

"Well, Dad came out, obviously. I don't remember anyone else."

"I've just remembered something," I announce. "Before Delia left that evening, I was looking out of the window, and I saw someone standing in front of the Lady Chapel. But it was dark and raining, and I couldn't tell who it was. When I looked again, they'd vanished. Sorry, I'd forgotten."

"Do you know if it was a man or a woman?" Imogen asks.

"No, sorry. I thought it was strange because it was raining and they were just standing there."

"Hmm," she says. "Okay. Well, thanks everyone. I'd better get a move on."

I walk out with her, trying not to look up at the knight as we pass. Outside, she bends to stroke Merlin, who wags his tail and licks her hand.

"Where are you off to now?" I ask her.

She straightens and sips her latte. "I need to speak to Christian."

"Oh." I grin. "Don't forget to put on a bit of lip gloss."

"It's not a social call," she says.

My smile fades. "You're questioning him?"

"We didn't finish our conversation the other night."

"You can't truly think he's involved with Liza's death?"

She shrugs. "Someone killed her. And it was almost certainly someone who knew her. Christian has access to fishing line."

"So does half of Glastonbury."

"He's also organizing an exhibition on the Tudors, and Liza's Tudor rose pendant was taken."

"That doesn't mean anything," I say softly.

She hesitates. "Will you come with me?"

"Of course, if you want me to. Wouldn't you rather have one of your officers?"

"I don't want to seem as if I'm coming on too heavy." She meets my eyes. "I can't not question him because I think he's sexy."

My lips curve up. "I knew you liked him."

"Of course I like him. But I can't, Gwen, not until this is sorted out."

"I understand. Hold on, I'll just tell Delia where I'm going." I nip into the café. When I come out, Imogen's putting on some lip gloss.

"Don't say a word," she growls.

"I wouldn't dream of it." I hide a smile as we begin walking down the street.

Within a couple of minutes, we're entering the library. We walk through to the reading room, then cross it to enter the museum offices.

Christian is in his office, sitting talking to Francis Sullivan, the Museum's Chief Executive. Francis looks exactly how you'd think the head of a museum would look. In his late fifties, he wears a tweed jacket and a shirt with a bow tie, and he speaks with a very posh English accent.

"Good afternoon, Detective Chief Inspector," he says to Imogen as she walks in, and, "Hello, Gwen," to me. "What can I do for you?"

"Actually, it's Mr. Wheeler I've come to see," Imogen says.

"Of course," Francis replies. He glances at her latte. "In the future, I'd be grateful if you didn't bring beverages into the library."

"Oh." She stares at the cup in her hand. "Sorry."

"Sets a bad example for customers, you know?"

"Of course. I apologize."

He heads out. Christian gives us an amused look. "He's a stickler for the rules," he says. "He made such a fuss last week at the Brue fishing competition when he discovered the winner had used an illegal bait."

"Francis goes fishing?" Imogen says.

Christian nods. "Most of us in the offices do. It's a good way to relax. I haven't been for months, though. I'm terrible at it. I never catch anything."

I glance at Imogen, hoping she sees that as a good sign. Her lips are pursed thoughtfully. She wants to believe he's innocent, but I know she's wrangling with herself.

"Do you believe in astrology?" I ask him.

He laughs. "That I share the same fate as a twelfth of the world's population? I don't think so."

I glance at her again. That has to be a good sign, right?

"Hmm," Imogen says. She's nervous again. She's sucked off most of her lip gloss, and she's clutching her coffee cup so tightly the cardboard is bending beneath her fingers. I hover awkwardly, wanting to give her moral support.

I return my gaze to Christian, wondering whether he's annoyed that she's clearly treating him like a suspect, but he's smiling gently. "What would you like to ask me?" he says.

"I'd just like to clarify some details about the night of the seventeenth," she replies.

"Okay." He looks over his glasses at her.

She clears her throat. "You told me you were here from five until six o'clock."

"That's right."

"You didn't mention that you left the office and went to your car."

"That was *before* five o'clock," he says smoothly. "I didn't think it mattered, as I came straight back."

"A witness saw you running to the car."

"That was Cooper," he says.

"Yes. You told him you left something in there."

"My laptop. I was due to have a conference call at five. I'd been working on photographs for the new exhibition all afternoon, and I didn't realize I didn't have my laptop. I was just about to set it up for the call and I realized I'd left it in the car. It was quite an important meeting with the British Museum, and I didn't want to be late, hence the running."

"Okay," she says.

"I swear I'm telling the truth," he says, giving her a small smile. "When I came back, I was soaking wet and late. I bumped into the table by the door, and I knocked over the vase on it. Luckily it was empty and plastic, so it just fell off and rolled down between the bookstacks. I didn't have time to pick it up, and then I forgot about it. You probably saw it when you came in," he says to me.

Imogen looks at me. I frown. "I don't remember seeing it." I give him an apologetic look. "I'm really sorry."

He and Imogen study each other for a long while. I hold my breath, sensing a poignant moment.

"The flowers were for my sister," he says eventually.

Imogen's eyebrows rise.

"The bouquet," he murmurs. "The one you saw Mary giving me yesterday. My sister's just had a baby. The flowers were for her."

Imogen tucks a loose strand of hair behind her ear. "Okay. I'll note that down."

"I'm telling the woman," he says softly. "Not the DCI."

Imogen blushes. Smiling, I slip out of the office and leave them to talk.

I'm walking slowly back through the library when she catches up with me.

"Well?" I ask her.

"Well, what?"

"Did he ask you out?"

"That would be inappropriate, considering he's a suspect."

"Aw," I say, "Immi…"

"He did," she says, and smiles. "And I said no, not until the case is solved."

"He was okay with that?"

"He was fine. He understands."

I stop and give her a hug. She laughs and hugs me back.

"We need to find who did this," she says, somewhat fiercely.

"I know."

"Not just because I want to date Christian Wheeler. But for Luke, and for the town."

"I know. We'll find him."

She releases me, and we head through the bookstacks.

I stop by the front door. "I wonder who picked up the vase Christian knocked off? The murderer?"

"Possibly," she replies. "I'll ask around, see if anyone admits to it."

"All right. I'll see you tomorrow?"

"Yeah. Have a great evening."

We part outside, and she heads off to her car, while I return to the café.

It's late afternoon. Cooper's already left, and Delia's starting to wipe down the tables as the last customers finish their tea and scones. I slip by the knight, sure I can feel his gaze on me as I go into the kitchen and start tidying up. Soon, though, I'm engrossed in the task, washing the pans, emptying the dishwasher and filling it again, wiping down the work benches, and getting everything ready for the next day.

Delia finishes her tasks, collects her coat, and waves goodbye. She goes out, and I see her walk across to her car, get in, and drive away.

I go over to the door and let Merlin in, then lock the door behind him. I need to sweep the floor and wipe down the counter, but I'm too nervous. Instead, I stand in front of the knight.

"Arthur," I whisper, "are you there?"

I blink, and there are the blue eyes, staring at me from behind the visor. "I'm here," he says.

I expected it, and deep down, even though I wouldn't admit it to myself, I hoped he'd appear, but my heart still skips a beat.

"Shall I take off the helm?" I ask him.

"Turn off the light first."

I flick the switch, leaving the break room light on, and return to him. Then I undo the catch of the helm, lift it off, and place it on the table.

He blows out a breath. "It's warm in there."

I back up a little and perch on the edge of the table behind me. His dark hair is sticking up on top. The grey streaks at the sides look like wings. He must have spent most of his time outdoors, because his face is tanned and slightly weather-beaten. I kept telling myself he couldn't possibly be as handsome as I remember, but I was wrong. He's gorgeous.

I've been thinking about talking to him all day, and now I don't know where to start. What on earth do you say to your knight in shining armour when he turns out to be real?

Chapter Ten

"How are you?" Arthur asks.

"I'm okay, thank you." I think he's referring to what happened at the Abbey. "Were you watching me? With Luke?"

"Yes. He looked upset."

"He was. That's why I hugged him." I don't know why I feel I have to explain myself.

"I understand," Arthur says. "You loved him. You wanted to make him feel better."

You loved him. Suddenly I realize the implication behind that statement. "You know that I dated him," I state. He nods. Oh… I think back to all the moments that have happened in this café, moments that Arthur must have witnessed. He told me, *I've been watching you since you were born.* He's seen me as a baby, as a child, as a girl growing into a young woman. He's watched my life unfold. This was where I first introduced Luke to Mum when I brought him home. He came here often in the first year at university when we were on vacation. I kissed him here. It's also where I came to tell Mum when he broke up with me. Where I sat and cried my heart out. And it's where I sat and cried again when Mum died.

"Why have you never shown yourself before now?" I ask, emotion tightening my throat. "There were so many times I could have done with comfort, with help…"

"I don't know," he says. "I haven't been aware, the way I am now. I was present, but also not…" He frowns. "I know that doesn't make any sense."

"It sort of does. It sounds as if your experience has been like coming out of a coma. Gradually becoming more conscious."

"Maybe."

We study each other in the quiet room. Merlin sits in front of me, wagging his tail at the knight. Arthur glances at him and smiles.

"I'm sorry I ran off the other day," I tell him.

"That's okay. I think you're very understanding, considering."

"I have some questions."

"It would be very strange if you didn't."

"First of all," I say, "how come I can understand you? Why aren't you speaking whatever language you spoke back then?"

"I'm… not sure. My world has… faded, over the years. I listen to your customers and friends, to the radio, and I watch TV. I suppose that's helped."

I glance over my shoulder at the small TV set. I sometimes put it on in the afternoons, and the radio is nearly always on.

"You look nice today," he says.

I look down at myself. I'm wearing a short denim skirt and a white T-shirt. My hair is in its usual scruffy bun. "I'm hardly dressed to the nines," I say.

"You'd look beautiful no matter what you wore."

I look back up at him, my face warming. "Don't say things like that."

"Sorry," he says.

"No, you're not."

"No, I'm not."

"Don't say things you don't mean," I scold.

"All right." He smiles.

When he smiles, I get a tingle all the way down my spine. It makes me feel tongue-tied, like Imogen was with Christian. I should have made a list of questions to ask him.

It occurs to me that he can't have had anything to eat or drink for fifteen hundred years. "Are you hungry? Or thirsty?"

"No." He shifts inside the armour, as if he's trying to roll his shoulders.

"Can you take the suit off?" Suddenly, more than anything, I want to see what he looks like without the steel plates strapped to him. As nice as it is, I want to see more than just his head.

But he just shakes it. "I don't think so. I'm not quite… ready."

"Beatrix—my aunt—says she thinks your soul is tied to the ruby, not the suit. She thinks we might be able to remove it and have it fitted into a piece of jewellery you can wear."

He looks at the pommel. "Really?"

"Would you like me to try it?"

"Yes," he says. "When we've finished talking."

"Okay." I'm happy to have a conversation, but I know I'm not doing very well at it. I feel a little shy, like he's a famous movie star.

I realize I'm slowly coming to the conclusion that he is who he says he is. Well, he's obviously magical. He can appear and disappear at will. I suppose it is possible he's a malevolent spirit who's here to do me harm, but my instincts tell me that's not the case. And as my instincts are pretty much all I have, I'm going to have to listen to them.

"You really are Arthur," I say.

"I am."

"Arthur, *Dux Bellorum.*"

He laughs for the first time, a sexy chuckle that rumbles in his chest. "Yes," he says. "Leader of battles. That is a good title."

"Not king."

"No, not king."

"But you are aware of the legend of King Arthur? That you're famous across the world?"

"The world?"

"Everyone knows who King Arthur is," I say softly. "There are so many books and movies about you."

"You shouldn't say that. If my head gets any bigger, it won't fit in this helm."

I laugh, and he smiles. "You don't laugh enough," he says.

I ignore the compliment, because it makes my tummy feel funny. "How much of the legend is true?"

"Not much, I'm afraid." He gives me a rueful smile. "I don't want to disappoint you."

"I'm talking to the man who did his best to remount the Roman cavalry, re-man the Saxon Shore forts, and keep Britannia safe for many years. I can't imagine how you could possibly disappoint me."

Ooh, he liked that. His smile is warm, making me turn to caramel inside.

I turn my attention to the Labradoodle who's sitting in front of me, looking up adoringly at the knight. "So was Merlin real?"

"I'm afraid not."

"So he's not a reincarnation of him. Aw, what a shame." I lean forward and ruffle the dog's ears.

But Arthur says, "Not of a mythical wizard, no. But he was one of my closest friends."

I stare at him. "You're kidding me?"

"You told me not to say things I didn't mean."

"You're serious?"

"Of course." He looks at the dog. Then he laughs. "Just a bit."

"Just a bit, what?"

His eyebrows rise. "He said he thinks we've shocked you."

I blink. "What do you mean? Who said that?"

"Merlin. You can't hear him?"

"Of course I can't hear him. He's a dog."

"I can hear him," Arthur says. "Must be a magic thing."

"Seriously? You can hear Merlin speak?"

"He has a nice voice. And he's a great poet."

"A poet?" Now I feel as if I'm going mad.

"His name was Taliesin," Arthur says. "But he's happy with Merlin."

I've heard of the bard Taliesin. There are rumours that he sang at Arthur's court. And now his spirit is in my dog? Merlin looks up at me with his big brown eyes, then nuzzles my hand. Am I crazy to believe all this?

And yet, what other explanation is there for the man inside the suit of armour who can disappear at will?

I look up at him. He's waiting patiently for me to process this new information.

"There is something I have to ask you," I say.

"Ask away."

"The stories about Guinevere and Lancelot... about them being, you know, lovers... were they real?"

His gaze holds mine, and it's firm and unrelenting. "Absolutely not. As I said, I had many advisers and warriors. But I was faithful to Guinevere, and she was faithful to me. We were in love. We had no need to look elsewhere for companionship."

I hadn't realized until that moment how nervous I was about his reply to that question. I've always hated the stories about Guinevere cheating on her king with his favourite knight. "You say 'she,'" I note, somewhat jokingly, "not 'you.' Have you changed your mind about me being a reincarnation of your Guinevere?"

"Not at all. I know saying that makes you uncomfortable, though." He sighs. "I've been thinking about it a lot since the last time we talked, and you were right. I can't expect everything to return to the way it was. Even if you are, at root, the same soul, you're not the same person you once were. You have no memory of our previous life, and how we felt about each other. It would be arrogant of me to think that nothing would change."

"Thank you." I'm relieved he understands.

"I will just have to win you all over again."

My mouth opens, but no words come out. He gives a small, mischievous smile.

I clear my throat. "What if I don't want that?"

He sighs patiently. "Then I'll go on my merry way and be the saddest man in the kingdom. I'm not a fool, Gwen. I'm not expecting anything. But expecting and hoping aren't the same thing. And I hope you'll come to see what a wonderful, amazing, irresistible, modest man I am."

I can't tell if he's joking. "Are you teasing me?" I ask suspiciously.

"I am. I'm very dry."

I look at Merlin. Arthur laughs. "He said you're going to have to get used to my sense of humour."

Merlin's tail wags vigorously from side to side. "Does he mind being a dog?" I ask.

"He doesn't like dog food much," Arthur says. "But apart from that I think he quite enjoys it."

I shake my head slowly, not sure if I can take all of this in. "So where do we go from here?" I ask softly.

"I've no idea."

"Do you know why you've become more aware? Why you've come back?"

"No."

"Is it to save England again?"

"I don't think so," he says gently. "I think it was you, Gwen. Seeing your sadness, your need… it brought me back to life."

We study each other for a long time. I like his manner. He's so calm and composed. I don't want to admit it, but I love the thought that he came back for me. What girl wouldn't find that romantic?

"I saw something odd yesterday," I tell him.

"Oh, what?"

I describe the twelve astrological glyphs visible around where Liza died. "I don't know what they mean, though," I admit. "But I also saw her ghost, and so did Merlin."

His eyebrows rise. "Really?"

"In the library. Luke saw her, too."

"Hmm. That's not good. It means her spirit has been unable to move on to the higher planes."

"Like yours?"

He tips his head from side to side. "Maybe."

"You think someone created a soulstone for her?"

"Possibly. Or maybe it's some other kind of magic that's keeping her here."

"How much do you know about magic?" I ask him.

"A little. Morgana used to talk to me about her abilities."

"I wish I was a real witch," I say.

He smiles. "You are."

"I make muffins, Arthur. I'm not exactly all, you know, abracadabra and stuff."

"Well, I think we both know real magic doesn't happen with the wave of a wand. And you are underplaying your skills. The ability to affect people's emotions with the food that you bake is no small thing. But you can do much more than that."

"I don't think so," I say doubtfully.

"Your abilities go back many, many generations," he says. "Maybe even to Morgana herself, who knows?" He surveys me thoughtfully. "Have you read your grandmother's journals?"

I stare at him. "What?"

"When she ran the café, she used to sit over there," he gestures with his head toward the corner by the window, "and write every night before she went home."

I'm astounded. "I didn't know that. I haven't seen anything she wrote."

"Maybe you could have a look in your mother's things and see if you can find them. They might give you an insight into what the astrological symbols mean."

"I will. Thank you."

"You're welcome."

I don't want to leave, but I'm tired, and Merlin needs feeding. "I should go now," I admit reluctantly.

"Of course," he says. "Are you going to take out the ruby?"

Oh yes, I'd forgotten about that. It's the moment of truth. Will I be able to make my knight in shining armour really come to life?

Chapter Eleven

I go over to the counter, extract the small tool bag I keep tucked in one of the cupboards, and take out a flat-headed screwdriver. Then I come back to Arthur.

"So... you want me to take out the ruby?" I ask him.

"Worth a try," he says.

I unscrew the lid of the pommel and lift a finger to the jewel inside. "What if it doesn't work?"

"I suppose you can just put it back."

"Are you sure? I don't want to lose you."

"You won't lose me."

"Are you certain about that?"

"I'm not going anywhere, Gwen. You're stuck with me now."

I reach out a hand and brush my thumb across his cheek. "You have stubble," I whisper.

"Do I?"

"You didn't have it yesterday."

"Hmm. You'd better get me out or my beard will end up curling out the bottom of my armour."

I'm only half listening; I can't believe I'm actually touching him. King Arthur. He's really alive.

"How old are you?" I ask softly.

"Thirty-three."

"I'm thirty later this year."

"I know. The twenty-third of September. I'll take you out to dinner to celebrate."

It doesn't surprise me at all that he knows my birthday. I look up into his eyes. "Can you do that?"

"I'll have to get out of the suit of armour first or everyone will stare. It's quite noisy."

"I mean, can you live a normal life? Will you be able to eat and drink? Will you age?"

"The stubble suggests so."

I rasp my thumb on it. I'm so full of hope, it's hard to breathe. He holds my gaze patiently, letting me study him. Then his gaze drops to my mouth. Oh my. He's thinking about kissing me.

Reluctantly, I move back a little. One step at a time.

"Okay," I tell him. "Here goes. Once it's out, I'll take it to the jewellery shop tomorrow and ask them to set it in a necklace or something."

"All right."

I insert the tip of the screwdriver in between the ruby and the claw of its setting. "Ready?"

"I trust you," he says.

I force the screwdriver in. It takes a few goes, but eventually the claw bends, the screwdriver slides behind the gem, and it pops out.

I catch it as it falls and look up.

Arthur's gone.

I swallow hard and look down at Merlin, feeling a sudden wave of panic. "What have I done?" I whisper. I know nothing about the soulstone and its links to the suit of armour. Maybe the two of them are bound together, and I've destroyed that link. "Has he gone forever?"

Merlin sneezes in a way that makes it look as if he's shaking his head. I give a short laugh and rub my nose. "All right. We'll stick to the plan, and hopefully it'll work."

I hold the ruby up. A beautiful rich red light spills from it onto my palm.

"Stay safe," I whisper. Then I slide the gem into my jeans pocket.

I've so much to think about, my head is aching a little. I screw the lid of the pommel back on and replace the knight's helm. Then I open the counter, take out one of my ginger cookies, and nibble it as I get my broom and sweep through the café. The cookies contain a simple relaxing spell, and sure enough, by the time I've finished sweeping and have wiped down the counter, my headache feels better.

When the café is clean, I turn off the lights, go out, and lock the door.

At home, I busy myself with getting dinner, then sit down to eat with a glass of wine. I put on the TV and switch it to the news, and have a couple of mouthfuls of dinner. Then I put down my plate. I look at Merlin, who's sitting watching me. I know it's not for food, because I never feed him off my plate.

"All right," I say softly. I slide my hand into my jeans pocket and bring out the ruby. Merlin comes over and sniffs it where it lies on my palm. I turn it, and it catches the light from the TV and winks at me.

"You can watch the news," I say, placing the gem on the coffee table. "The sport will be on in a minute. I wonder what kind of sport you like? I'm guessing you're not a darts kind of man."

Merlin opens his mouth to pant, for all the world as if he's laughing. I sit back with a smile and pick up my tray. I guess I'm going a little bit loopy, talking to a crystal and a dog. But for the first time in a long time, I don't feel so alone.

*

On Friday morning, I leave the café in Delia's capable hands and take a walk into town, Merlin at my side. Due to it being the site of the famous music festival, Glastonbury has gained a reputation for being the home of hippies and those interested in alternative religions and practices. This is reflected in its wide range of shops that sell colourful clothing and fancy painted boots, crystals and wind chimes, and herbs and wands. I love the eclectic mix of people here, and feel comfortable among those who, for whatever reason, don't feel they subscribe to the normal way of life.

There are 'normal' shops here, too: a post office, a bakery, a florist, a book shop, and also Mackenzie's Jewellery Shop, its front window displaying a wonderful mix of diamond engagement rings and pendants in the shape of oak leaves, pentacles, crosses, and the symbol for Om.

I go inside, leaving Merlin sitting on the pavement. It's quiet at this time of morning, and the shop is empty apart from the owner.

"Morning, Gwen!" It's James Mackenzie himself, in his sixties, with white hair and beard and a thick Scottish accent. "How are you, lassie?"

"I'm good, thank you, James. How are you?"

"Fine, lassie, fine. What can I do for you on this beautiful day?"

"I have a special task for you, if you choose to accept it." I slide my hand into my pocket, take out the ruby, and put it on my palm.

I feel a strong sense of reluctance as I hold it out. I don't want to let it go. But I've known James since I was a child, and I trust him to handle it with care.

"Oh my goodness," James says. I needn't have worried about him handling it, because he takes it gently, as if it's a snowflake and will disappear at any moment, and holds it on the palm of his hand as he peers at it. "Where did you get this?"

I'm suddenly aware I've pried it out of a museum piece that doesn't belong to me, and I try not to blush. "It's a family heirloom."

"It's beautiful." Carefully, he turns it over, then takes out an eyepiece and examines it closely. "It's an oval custom cut, pigeon-blood red, around five carats." He looks up at me. "Maybe worth around thirty thousand pounds."

My eyes nearly fall out and roll across the counter. "What?"

"It's beautiful, Gwen. I think it's Scottish. I've heard about them but never seen one." He peers into its depths. "It has a beautiful red glow."

He's silent for a full thirty seconds. Eventually, I clear my throat, and he looks up and blinks. "Sorry. It's quite mesmerising…"

"I'd like to give it as a present for a friend," I tell him softly. "Something he can wear. I was thinking a necklace?"

"Possibly." He turns it with his fingers. "It would make a better ring."

"A ring… what type?"

"For a man, you say?"

"Yes." I think about Arthur *Dux Bellorum*. A warrior. "He's a man's man. He's not used to wearing jewellery."

"Something simple, then. A plain gold band. The ruby nestled in the setting rather than riding high, so it's not easily knocked out."

"That sounds perfect," I say happily. "How much will it cost?"

"What size do you think it needs to be?"

I have no idea, but I explain that he's a big guy and has big hands, so James suggests a size that should fit one of Arthur's fingers, and says he'll happily resize it if it doesn't fit.

He names an approximate price to set the stone into the gold band, and I try not to wince. I don't have a lot of savings. But this is important. I can't leave Arthur trapped in the suit of armour.

"I can work on it over the weekend," James says. "It'll be ready Monday."

It's generous of him to do it so quickly, but even so, I don't like the thought of being parted from it for so long. But I smile and nod, and he writes me a receipt, then takes it out the back to his workshop.

I leave the shop and walk back up the high street toward the café. I look down at Merlin, trotting at my side. "I miss him already. Is that crazy?"

Merlin shakes his head and sighs. I feel a peculiar mixture of emotions. Loss and sadness, and also a bubbling excitement at the thought of what might happen when I get the ring back.

But first I have several days to get through. As I pass under the oak trees with their new leaves, I wonder how Imogen is doing with the murder enquiry. At that exact moment, my phone rings, and I see on the screen that it's her.

"I was just thinking about you," I say, smiling.

"Weird," she replies. "Anyone would think you had psychic powers or something."

I chuckle. "How's it going? Caught him yet?"

"I'm working on it. What are you up to? I called in for a chat, but Delia said you'd gone into town."

"I'm on my way back." I watch Merlin snuffling along the ground. I'm not sure whether to tell Imogen about Arthur and the ruby. She's very open minded about me being a witch, but I don't know what she'll think about soulstones and King Arthur hiding in my suit of armour. I decide to keep it to myself, for now. "Just picking up a few bits for the weekend," I tell her. "It was quiet in the café and I felt like stretching my legs."

"Fair enough." She pauses. "Are you… you know… okay?"

My eyebrows rise. "What do you mean?"

"Finding a dead body would have freaked anyone out. But finding the body of an old school friend, someone you knew well and had a history with, and the fact that she's not just dead but murdered… it would be no surprise if you were struggling a bit with it."

"I'm okay," I tell her, touched by her concern.

"Alice only died six months ago," she says softly. "I know how hard it's been for you to adjust to losing her."

I stop walking and watch Merlin snuffling happily at the roots of a tree. "Yes, it has been hard. But I'm okay."

"Are you sure? Are you going to talk to a therapist or something? I'm worried about you."

"Why? Honestly, I'm okay."

"It's just… everyone thinks you've been a bit distracted, and… don't blame Delia… but she said she overheard you talking to Sir Boss."

"You talk to him all the time," I say, amused.

"Yes, but I'm bonkers. You're the sane one. You've always put everyone else first your whole life. I'm not sure you know how to do anything for yourself." She hesitates. "You're very important to me, Gwen. You keep me grounded. I… look up to you, and I admire you."

Her words startled me. "Gosh."

"We've always told each other everything. I can't begin to understand your magical talents, but I love that you're a witch, and I'd hate anything to happen to you." She sounds a little tearful, very unlike my best friend.

I frown. "Immi, what's happened?"

"Nothing. Well, almost nothing. It's just… it's Matthew Hopkins."

I go cold. "What's he done?"

"He's put in a formal complaint about you. He said you cursed him."

I laugh. "I wish I could. I'd make him go bald or something. That would show him. But I can't. Or at least, I'd never do that. I only do positive spells, Immi—my cakes cure headaches and make people feel more positive for a few hours. I thought you knew that."

"I do… I just wondered whether what's happened had tipped you over the edge, and now I feel terrible even thinking you'd do anything like that."

"It's okay."

"It's not. I'm so sorry."

"Immi, it's your job. You have to question everything and everyone." For the first time, I wonder what kind of an impact the investigation is having on her. Liza was hardly a good friend of ours, but Immi's had to question Christian, and all her other friends.

Suddenly suspicious, I ask, "Have you discovered something about someone we know? I mean, I know you can't tell me any details, but I wondered if that's what's bothering you."

She doesn't say anything for a moment. Then she says, "What are you up to tomorrow night?"

"Uh… nothing. Why?"

"You want to go for a drink? I could do with a girly night out."

"I'd love to. I'm going to look through my books tonight and see if I can find anything out about the astrological signs around Liza's body."

"Excellent. You can tell me if you've found anything out tomorrow."

"All right."

"I'll knock on your door at seven," she says. "We'll walk down to the Lady of the Lake." It's our local pub, which is great because we can both have a drink and we don't have to drive home, as she lives not far from me.

"Perfect," I tell her. "I'll see you then. And Immi?"

"Hmm?"

"I'm all right, honestly."

"I'm glad. Just… steer clear of Hopkins, okay?"

"You don't have to convince me of the wisdom of that."

"Good. See ya." She hangs up.

I walk slowly back to the café, Merlin at my side. Something's bothering her, something she can't tell me about.

Briefly, I wish Arthur was with me, watching over me. But there's nothing I can do about that now.

I reach the café, push open the door, and go inside into the warm interior that smells of coffee and lemon muffins. I have a day's work ahead and lots to do, and I put everything else to the back of my mind.

Chapter Twelve

It turns out there are several coachloads of tourists visiting the Abbey and the Adventure in the afternoon, so I'm flat out from lunchtime onward. By the time the evening comes and I get home, I'm shattered. I think the emotional turmoil of the past week is finally taking its toll. I decide to get a fish and chip takeaway and eat it with a beer while I watch an action movie that takes up no brain power, but I thoroughly enjoy. By nine p.m., I'm in bed and asleep, Merlin curled up in the doorway, keeping guard.

We open the café on Saturdays, but although I go in to bake a few rounds of sausage rolls and muffins, by lunchtime I'm done, and I leave the café in Delia's hands. She'll have Monday afternoon off instead. I head home with the luxurious feeling of having a whole afternoon and Sunday off.

This weekend it's the spring equinox, one of the two times of year when the hours of day and night are equal all over the planet. It's the pagan festival of Ostara, and one of my favourite celebrations. The Christian festival of Easter isn't for another few weeks, but the two have a similar theme of renewal and rebirth.

Today, after a sandwich and a cup of tea, I spend a few hours working in the garden. I have a veggie patch and herb garden, as well as several flower borders and a greenhouse. I weed the vegetable beds and dig some compost into them, sow some carrots, broad beans, peas, and onions, and plant some mint, basil, thyme, and sage. Tomorrow I'll sow lettuce and tomatoes in the greenhouse, and plant some summer bulbs—lilies, gladioli, and agapanthus—in the borders, and I'll do some spring cleaning indoors.

I bring out a new pack of bottles of water, take the bottles out of the plastic wrap, and line them up on the outside table, ready to be blessed under the full moon.

By this time, it's late afternoon, the sky is clouding over, and I feel the first few drops of rain, so I retire inside. I spend some time reading about various herbs and spices, then plan out some new recipes that I hope will help people with various ailments.

Cinnamon lowers blood sugar and cholesterol levels, so I come up with a new recipe for some spiced toffee cookies that I'll make in the café on Monday. Turmeric is another spice that has anti-inflammatory properties and is good for arthritis, and I create a recipe for turmeric carrot muffins—I'll add a spell to them to take away pain. Basil helps reduce stress, so I invent a bacon, pesto, and sundried tomato muffin, and I'll top that up with a relaxation spell.

By now it's raining and a little gloomy, but I cheer myself up with a cup of herbal tea and a Twix. After my rest, I lower the ladder to the loft, switch on the light, and climb up.

I don't come up here often, but it's relatively clean and free of dust. I don't have a garage, so this is my storage room, and there are quite a few boxes here taped and piled up. Mine are at the front, my mother's are behind, and there are even older ones at the back that I'm sure belonged to my grandmother.

I begin moving aside the ones at the front containing some of Mum's old kitchen equipment that I don't use every day but have kept in case I need it. Then there are memory boxes—they contain old schoolbooks of mine that Mum kept, a shawl from when I was born, an old sweater of my father's. I press my nose into it; it still retains the slight scent of his aftershave. Beneath it is a photo of the two of them with me as a baby at a beach somewhere—I turn it over, and on the back Mum's written Alice, John, and Gwen at Bigbury Bay, Devon, 1993. I was two years old. Just a year later, my father would pass away, killed in a car crash in London.

Not wanting to get bogged down in the past, I place it back and move the box to one side.

Behind it are a couple of boxes of photos. I shift those and climb into the space behind. I look through Mum's clothes I haven't been able to bring myself to get rid of, some of her jewellery, more photos, mementoes from holidays, all sorts of things.

I keep moving and shifting boxes, until eventually I see some boxes marked Lizzie—my grandmother's name.

My pulse picks up speed a little. I pull one of the photo boxes forward so I can sit on it, then drag the first of Lizzie's boxes toward me.

There are more photos here—of Lizzie and Richard, my grandfather, my mother and Beatrix when they were young, on holidays, at school, and in the garden of this house. And then older photos beneath those. On the back, Lizzie has written names in her loopy handwriting, the photos are of her and her siblings with her parents and grandparents, going back generations.

I brush a thumb over a picture of Mum and Beatrix as babies with Lizzie, my grandmother, Harriet, my great-grandmother, and Josephine, my great-great-grandmother, smiling as I think how Matthew Hopkins would have a fit seeing all these witches. But this isn't why I came up here, so, leaving that one photo out, I replace the rest and move them aside, then start searching through the boxes at the back.

And that's when I find it. Beneath another box, in the corner, a small wooden chest. I've never seen it before.

I remove the boxes around it and pull it forward. My fingers tingle and for some reason, beneath me at the bottom of the stepladder, Merlin barks.

There's a catch on the front. It's locked.

I purse my lips, frustrated. Do I have the key? Please, don't let it be in one of the other boxes…

Then I remember that, in the kitchen, in the bottom drawer, there's a box of odd keys. I've never figured out where they go, but it's Sod's Law that if I throw them out, I'll need them the next day.

With some difficulty, I manoeuvre the chest across to the top of the stepladder. It's not easy to get boxes down on my own, but luckily some time ago I fashioned a clever device out of rope, and I use it now, fitting the box into the harness, then lowering it down the steps as carefully as I can. Merlin is very excited and dances around it as I turn off the light, then climb down the stepladder, lowering the hatch behind me.

"It might not be what we're looking for," I tell him as I pick the chest up and carry it into the kitchen. "It might contain Lizzie's old socks or something." But I have to admit I'm breathing quickly, excited at the thought that this might be the one.

After opening the bottom drawer, I take out the bowl of keys and begin sorting through them. There are rusty keys that look like they unlock shed padlocks, old door keys, tiny keys for bike locks, keys to suitcases, all sorts. And then, at the bottom, I find an old, ornate key that looks just the right size.

Breathless, I take it out, insert it in the lock of the chest, and turn it.

It opens.

I lift the latch, then open the chest.

Inside are about thirty books. They're all shapes and sizes, some with hard covers, some paperbacks. I take one out. To my surprise, I realize it was my mother's. On the front it has her name, Alice Young, and it's illustrated with flowers and stars. I scan the front of the other books, my jaw dropping as I see the names. Alice Young. Lizzie Brown. Then underneath, Harriet Tucker—my great-grandmother. And right at the bottom, Josephine Fox. My great-great-grandmother.

Oh my Goddess. These are Books of Shadows. All witches have these. Sometimes we use them as diaries or journals, recording our day-to-day practices, at other times they're for listing the ingredients for spells, for writing down research into herbs and crystals, or merely for transcribing our thoughts on festivals and practices. I've amassed a few over the years, and I have a couple of my mother's, which I've devoured. But I hadn't realized all these existed.

I take out the book right at the bottom. It's one of Josephine's, dated 1928. I know she was born in 1899, so that would make her the same age as me when she wrote this. I open it carefully and leaf through the pages. It's a recipe book, and it also has pages recording the benefits of various herbs she's discovered. Alongside the recipes are spells to enhance the herbs' properties.

"Oh, Merlin…" I sink to the floor and bury my face in Merlin's fur as he comes up to sit beside me. I knew that my mother and grandmother used baking to do their magic, but I never realized it went back this far, and maybe even further. Perhaps it goes back as far as the first Alice Young in the seventeenth century. Or maybe even as far back as Morgana.

I'm no longer able to talk to the women in my family, but through their journals and the beauty of witchcraft I can still connect with them and use their skills to further my own.

"I'm all right," I tell Merlin as he whines and licks my face, and I realize there are tears on my cheeks. "Come on." I get to my feet and pick up the chest. "Let's go in the living room. It's warmer in there."

I spend a couple of hours reading through the journals. Then I stop and make myself some dinner—pasta tonight, with a lamb ragout and some herb bread. My mind dips and whirls like a kite in the wind as I eat, thinking about my family, and about Arthur. I wonder how James is getting on with making the ring? Will it mean Arthur can escape the suit of armour? I look down at Merlin, who's stretched out on his side in front of the fire, dozing. Is he truly an old friend of Arthur's? Or am I going crazy?

Knowing there are no answers, I take my plate out and wash it up, then check the time. I have thirty minutes or so until Immi's due to call. I nip upstairs and change, brush my hair and braid it, slick on a bit of lip gloss, then return downstairs.

Merlin is sitting at the bottom of the stairs with one of the journals in his mouth.

I stare at him. "Oh! What are you doing with that?" I bend and take it from where he's holding it tenderly in his jaws. It's one of my great-great-grandmother's. I look at Merlin. "Why did you pick this one?"

He sneezes in response.

I go into the living room and perch on the edge of the sofa, then leaf through the book slowly. It looks much the same as the others. Recipes, notes, jottings, the occasional picture. I can't imagine why he's singled this one out.

Then I turn the page and my eyes nearly fall out of my head. Neatly drawn on the page are the twelve astrological symbols, and at the top are written the words, 'The Star Sign Spell.'

Chapter Thirteen

When the doorbell sounds, I open the front door to see Imogen standing there, looking gorgeous in jeans and a pretty blue blouse beneath a long black coat. She's released her hair from its usual tight bun, and it hangs around her shoulders in brown waves. She's also carrying a beautiful bouquet of spring flowers—peonies, roses, tulips, freesias…

To my surprise, she holds it out to me. "Happy Ostara," she says.

I'm so touched that she understands the importance of the day that my eyes fill with tears.

"You're not going to cry, are you?" she asks suspiciously, even though her own eyes shine as I take the flowers.

"Of course not," I say in a squeaky voice. "They're beautiful. Thank you so much. I'll just pop them in some water." I go back inside, run a few inches of water into my washing up bowl, and lie the flowers carefully on the sink so the ends sit in the water. Later, I'll take time to arrange them in a vase. "That's so thoughtful," I tell Imogen, who's bending to kiss Merlin's head.

"I know it's a special day for you," she says. "It was the least I could do. Mary had some amazing bouquets in the florist shop. It was tough to choose."

"They're gorgeous. I've never seen such big roses." It really feels as if spring is on the way now.

"You look lovely tonight," she says as we go into the hallway. "I love the colour of your hair. It's so much more interesting than my muddy brown colour."

I glance at myself in the hall mirror. The light above me shines on my red hair, giving it gold highlights. Tonight, I look as if I belong in Glastonbury. I'm wearing a floor-length green skirt, with a tie-dyed top in blue and green. I could easily be the witch in Beatrix's painting. "Thought I'd jazz things up a bit. Anyway, you look gorgeous too, as always. It's nice to see you out of a suit."

"Feels odd. Not sure if I like it."

Smiling, I lead the way out of the house and close the door behind us.

We start walking down to the Lady of the Lake, Merlin trotting beside us. It's dark, and the streetlights cast golden circles on the ground. I think of the festival, of the fact that it's the birth of new things, and something springs into my mind. "Have you heard from Christian?"

"Why do you say that?"

"I was just thinking about his sister having a baby, and I wondered how it was."

"You freak me out the way you do that," she says. "I bumped into him this morning. The baby's not well. She has an... um... Atrial Septal Defect."

"A hole in the heart?"

"That's right. Apparently, as a baby's heart develops, there are several openings in the wall that divides the upper chambers of the heart, but they usually close during pregnancy or after the baby's born. But Cassie's—that's what they've called the baby girl—haven't closed. She has a heart murmur, and she's having difficulty breathing."

"Oh no, Immi... Can anything be done?"

"They will do surgery if they have to, but they want to wait a few days to see how she does because she's so small." She bends her head, and her hair swings down to hide her face.

"How's Christian?" I ask softly.

"Worried out of his mind, of course." She hesitates. "Is there anything you can do?"

My eyebrows rise. "Magically, you mean?"

"Mm."

Although I'm a witch and a pagan, Imogen knows I'm interested in lots of other religions and practices. Most religions feature some form of faith or spiritual healing, and although the main way I do my spells is through cooking, I also sometimes practice a form of spiritual healing.

"I don't have any great skill," I tell her gently. "I can sometimes help a headache or ease a tight chest, but I can't cure serious illnesses."

Unbidden, I hear Arthur's voice in my head, then, saying *You can do much more than that.* Hmm. Where did that come from?

I clear my throat. "Anyway, I don't like doing direct healing without the permission of the recipient."

"Can I ask Christian?"

I frown. I see the guy frequently at the museum. He was dismissive of astrology; he might think me ridiculous and laugh in my face next time he sees me.

I lift my chin. If he does that, then he's not worth my time. "Of course," I tell her. "I'd be happy to help if he and his sister wants."

"Okay." She doesn't say anything more.

"So what else have you been up to today?" I ask her.

"Going through the evidence from the library and trying to come up with a hypothesis for the murder."

"And have you?"

"No. Don't tell my boss."

I smile and hold the door of the pub open for her. She goes in and Merlin follows her, knowing he's allowed inside. I go after them and let the door swing shut behind me.

It's warm inside—flames are leaping in the grate, and the room is busy. I know most of the people present. Cooper's there with a couple of mates, and he waves hello. Christian is standing at the end of the bar talking with another guy around his own age; he nods as he sees us, and Imogen gives a casual, I-see-you-but-I-don't-really-care-that-you're-here kind of nod back. To my disappointment, I also glimpse Matthew Hopkins, playing pool in another room.

"Dammit," Imogen says. "Do you want to leave? Go to the pub down the road?" She knows that Matthew has it in for me.

But I want a drink and I don't want to leave, so I shake my head and go up to the bar. We place an order—red wine for me, Scotch and Coke for her—and take them over to a free table by the window. A lone candle casts the table in a yellow glow. The pub smells of the malty aroma of beer and salt-and-vinegar crisps. I feel comfortable here, safe, if I forget about Matthew Hopkins.

"Christian looks nice," I say.

Imogen gives me a wry look and glances at him. "He's with his brother-in-law. Trying to take his mind off Cassie for a few minutes, I suppose." She has a large mouthful of her drink and sighs, then bends to stroke Merlin's ears. He closes his eyes in bliss. "Anyway, what have you been doing today?"

"Working in the garden, mainly. And then this afternoon, I made a very interesting discovery."

"Ooh, do tell."

I explain how I discovered the journals of the witches in my family, and the kind of things they contain. "And then, just before you came," I add, "I found something very important. It was in one of Josephine's journals—my great, great-grandmother. She was born before the turn of the previous century." I glance around to make sure nobody's watching, then lean closer to Imogen. "I found a page where she'd drawn all the astrological symbols in a circle."

Imogen's eyes widen. "What?"

"And in the middle, she'd written a spell that could be used. She called it The Star Sign Spell."

"What did it do?"

I take a deep breath. "It binds the soul of someone who's died to this plane."

She stares at me. "You mean Liza?"

"Yes. That's why we've seen her ghost. It's intense magic, and it would take someone with a lot of power to cast it."

"You're telling me our murderer is a witch?"

"Yes."

She sits back in her chair, stunned. "Does that mean it's a woman?"

"No, not necessarily. Witchcraft is all about balance, about the recognition of a god and a goddess. Women are often drawn to it because it recognizes the goddess and she is seen as the god's equal, but there are many male witches. Some people call them wizards or warlocks, but many men who follow the Craft just call themselves witches."

I sip my wine and let Immi study me thoughtfully. In essence, it doesn't help with her investigation at all. Even if it were to lead her to discover who committed the murder, she can hardly use the information in court to prosecute them. But if it helps us to discover who did it, it's still an important detail.

"How does the spell work?" she asks eventually.

"I'm not a hundred percent sure," I admit. "I've never dabbled in that kind of magic. Everything I do is focused on healing and light. To do any kind of curse, you have to draw on negative feelings—hate, fear, and resentment, that kind of thing, and I don't like doing that. The person who did this must have really hated Liza." I rub my nose.

"Well, obviously. I guess you don't murder someone unless you dislike them in some way."

Imogen gives a little nervous laugh at that, and that sets me off, and soon the two of us are giggling like fourteen-year-olds.

"It's not funny," she says eventually.

"Not at all." I wipe beneath my eyes. "It's really not."

"Care to share the joke?"

We both look up at the man's voice, and my heart sinks to see it's Matthew Hopkins. I hadn't heard him sneak up on us. Oh Goddess. How much of what I said did he hear?

Merlin barks, and I sink a hand into his fur.

"This is a private conversation," Imogen says icily. "And I'll thank you for not joining in without being invited."

He ignores her and turns his full attention on me. "So what kind of magic do you dabble in, Gwen?"

He did hear me. I squash down the feeling of panic that rises within me and glare at him. "I'm having a quiet drink with a friend. I'm not interested in conversing with the press."

"I heard you discussing the murder of Liza Banks," he says. He looks at Imogen for the first time. "I'm guessing you've questioned Miss Young and ruled her out of your enquiries."

"I'm not at liberty to discuss any undergoing investigation, *sir*."

"Gwen hated Liza," he continues. "I've interviewed several of their old school friends who were keen to discuss the animosity that Gwen bore for her."

"I bet they were," Imogen says. "Anything for their five minutes of fame."

"I didn't hate her," I protest.

Matthew's eyes narrow. "Even though she took your boyfriend?"

"She didn't take him. We'd already broken up."

"That's not what I heard," he says. "One of her closest friends told me she started dating Luke Mathers two months before you left the University of Exeter and moved back to Glastonbury."

Nausea rises inside me, and for a moment I think I'm going to vomit. Merlin growls and bares his teeth at the reporter. For a moment, I'm tempted to let him sink his teeth into the man. But Matthew would complain and demand to have the dog put down, so I restrain him.

Imogen gets to her feet. "Did you think I wouldn't read the article you published this morning?" she asks softly. Despite my shock, my eyebrows rise. What article?

Matthew's lips curve up in a nasty smile. "I wondered if you'd see it."

"Of course I saw it." She glances at me. "He wrote a summary of the investigation so far. Some of the highlights were 'inept police department,' 'incompetent officers,' and 'bungling detective chief inspector.'"

Matthew laughs.

Imogen's eyes narrow. "I've already asked you once to leave us alone," she states clearly, her voice ringing across the room. "If you don't move away from the table now, sir, I promise I will make you do so forcefully." She's putting on her DCI voice. I would've laughed if I wasn't so upset.

"Need some help?" Christian ambles up to us, his voice casual, although his eyes are hard.

"Mr. Hopkins was just leaving," Imogen states.

"I really wasn't," Matthew says.

Christian glares at him. "You're drunk."

"And you're ugly, but in the morning I'll be sober."

"You're not fit to polish Winston Churchill's boots," Christian snaps, "let alone claim his sayings as your own. Get out before I throw you out."

I know that Imogen can cope perfectly well on her own; I've seen her manhandle men twice her size on more than one occasion. But she keeps quiet, and Matthew's gaze slides from her to Christian. She and Christian are both tall and look like they can handle themselves, and for the first time Matthew looks uncertain.

"I know you had something to do with Liza's death," he says to me. "And I'm determined to prove it." He turns on his heel, walks out, and lets the door bang behind him.

Everyone breathes out a sigh of relief. Imogen turns to me with a look of pity on her face.

"Gwen…"

"I'm all right." I speak brightly, even though I'm not.

"He just wants to hurt you," she says, looking pained because she knows I'm upset.

"I know. Don't worry about it."

"But—"

"Don't worry about it," I repeat, and she falls silent. I get to my feet. "I think I'll head home."

"Let me walk you," Christian says, but I shake my head.

"Merlin won't let anything happen to me." I'm already pulling on my jacket. Then I stop and rest a hand on his arm. "I'm very sorry to hear about baby Cassie. I hope she improves soon."

His expression softens. "Thank you."

I turn to Immi. "I'll see you later. Thanks again for the flowers."

"You're welcome."

We exchange a kiss, and then I leave them to it and walk out into the night.

I pause for a moment outside, making sure Matthew has left, but there's no sign of him. "Come on," I say to Merlin. "Let's go home."

We walk quickly up the hill to my house. I try not to think about anything, but it's impossible to stop Matthew's words ringing in my head. Is it true that Luke and Liza were already seeing each other before we broke up? I want to say no, but deep down, I know it's true.

I let myself into the house, close the door, and lock it behind me. Then I sag tiredly against the wall. Ultimately, what does it matter? It was years ago. Liza's dead, and I'm not in love with Luke anymore.

What does matter is that Matthew has new fuel for his theory, and I know he's got the bit between his teeth. He's convinced I'm a witch, and he's not going to stop until he proves it. I need to be more careful. It might not be the seventeenth century, and I'm not likely to be hanged for practising witchcraft, but who knows what damage it might do if the town gets to find out? My private life is exactly that—private, and I don't want everyone knowing my business.

I feel suddenly vulnerable indoors, knowing Matthew is out there, and so is the murderer. And that makes me cross. I'm not going to let other people make me feel uneasy in my own home.

I take off my jacket and boots, pour myself a glass of red wine, and curl up on the sofa. For once, I allow Merlin on the seat next to me, feeling the need for some company.

If Arthur were here, he could sit beside me. Maybe he'd put his arm around me, and we could snuggle down and watch TV together.

Keeping that dream in my head, I drink my wine and eventually doze off.

Chapter Fourteen

On Sunday morning, around ten a.m., Imogen rings. "It's me," she says. "How are you doing?"

"I'm fine." I don't tell her I spent most of the night awake, looking at the ceiling. "More importantly, how are you? Did you get to spend some time with Christian?"

"I did, as it happens. His brother-in-law went home and Christian and I had a drink together."

"Oh, lovely." I smile. She deserves to have a little romance in her life.

"We had a chat about you," she says.

My smile fades. "Oh. Hmm."

"All good things," she adds. "Christian wanted to know what Matthew was on about, so I took the plunge and told him."

"That I'm a witch?"

"Well, I started by saying that Matthew thinks you're a witch, to… you know… test the waters. He didn't collapse with laughter, so then I added that actually, Matthew's right."

"Did he faint?"

She laughs. "No. He did an exhibition on witchcraft earlier in the year, so he's done quite a bit of research on it."

"I remember that." I helped him with some of it.

"I think he would have been more scornful if I'd said you waved a wand and rode a broom, but when I explained how it's all about energy and intention, he was actually very interested."

I blow out a long breath. "I'm so glad."

"Me too. I told him that most of the work you do involves herbs and cooking, but that you also do some spiritual healing. And he says his sister, Rachel, is very open to alternative stuff, and, well, he'd like you to come to the hospital to meet her."

"Oh." I didn't expect that. "When?"

"Well, why not this morning? I can pick you up in thirty minutes?"

I know her well enough to hear the note of concern in her voice. "What's happened? Is Cassie okay?"

"Not really. She's taken a turn for the worse. So if there's anything you can do, well, I'm sure they'd appreciate it."

I hesitate for a moment. This is the kind of problem that witches have run into through the centuries. If I go to the hospital and attempt spiritual healing on the baby, and she takes a turn for the worse or— Goddess forbid—dies, it will be very easy for everyone to blame me. But I can't say no when there's a decent chance that I might be able to ease the child's suffering.

"Of course I'll come," I tell her.

"Thank you. I'll see you at half ten." She hangs up.

I sigh and start getting ready. This is the last thing I need really, with all the worry about Liza and Matthew Hopkins, but it's not Cassie's fault or her parents', and I want to help if I can.

At dead on ten thirty, Imogen knocks on the door, and soon we're on our way to the local hospital. I've left Merlin in the garden—he might well jump over the low wall at the bottom and wander off, but he always comes back by the end of the day.

"So what else did you and Christian talk about last night?" I ask her.

"Stuff," she says, and blushes.

I smile. "Have you agreed to go on a date with him?"

"Not until I've solved the case."

"What if you don't manage to?"

"I will," she states. "We're making inroads."

I don't know if she's referring to discovering the murderer is a witch, or if she's uncovered some other evidence. I know she doesn't feel comfortable discussing ongoing investigations, so instead I decide to raise the subject of something that's been on my mind.

"I've got something else to tell you," I announce. "It's not about the case."

"Okay. Fire away."

I clear my throat. "It's a bit weird."

"My dear Gwen, weird is your middle name. I'm used to it."

"I guess. Okay. You know Sir Boss?"

Her eyebrows rise. "Of course."

"Well, what if I told you that… um… there's a person living inside him?"

She stares at me for so long that for a moment I worry she's going to crash the car. She finally looks back at the road, her brow furrowed. "What do you mean? Someone's put on the suit and is living in the café?"

"Not quite. Have you heard of soulstones?"

"No."

I tell her what Beatrix told me—that the Celts are known for imprisoning souls inside gems or other objects, and then about the ruby I found inside the pommel of the sword. I finish with, "Beatrix thinks that's what's happened—that the ruby contains the man's soul."

"What man?" Imogen asks.

"His name is Arthur."

"You've spoken to him?"

"Yes. A few times."

"Sort of like a genie in the lamp."

"Yes, very much like that."

"Okay. So this Arthur's soul has been captured in a ruby, and he's slowly becoming more conscious and appearing inside the suit of armour."

"Yes, exactly." I tell her how I removed the ruby and have taken it into Mackenzie's Jewellery Shop. "I'm going to have it fitted in a ring, to see if that means Arthur can leave the suit of armour."

"I see." She glances at me and examines my face. I blush. Her lips curve up in a smile. "Aw," she says softly, "you're soft on this guy."

"No. Not at all. Not one jot. Okay, a little bit."

She's taking it all very well. I can't tell from her expression how much of it she believes. "How long's he been in the ruby?" she asks.

"Um… I think around fifteen hundred years."

She's quiet for a very long time. I look out the window at the flat marshy fields of the Somerset levels, wondering how Arthur's doing in the jewellery shop.

Eventually she says, "So he was put into the ruby around the year 500."

"Yes."

"My history's not great, but that's after the Romans left Britain."

"Yes. They left in 410."

"And then the Anglo-Saxons came."

"And a few Jutes and Frisians—lots of Germanic tribes. It's what we call the Dark Ages because we know so little about it."

"What happened to the Celts? That's who were here before the Romans, right?"

"Yes. We call them the Romano-British after the Romans left. They were pushed west into Wales and Cornwall when the Anglo-Saxons invaded."

"They just rolled over and let them invade?"

"Well, no. They kept them at bay for a long time. They were led by a man, a warrior, who tried to learn from the Romans. He trained his warriors in Roman tactics, and he had a cavalry, and he kept the old Saxon Shore forts manned on the coast. He was an amazing leader."

"Oh no."

"Immi…"

"You're saying the dude in the suit of armour is that Arthur?"

"Yes," I finish lamely.

"King Arthur?"

"Well, he wasn't a king, he was a military leader…"

"That's the most amazing story I've ever heard," she says. "Oh my God, Gwen, please tell me you're not playing with me."

I laugh, feeling almost tearful at her reaction. "No, I'm not. Beatrix says it's possible. And… well… you have to talk to him to see it for yourself, but he's not just like any normal guy. He's different somehow. I can totally believe he was an ancient warrior who commanded whole armies."

"Can I meet him?"

"I hope so. I'm picking the ring up tomorrow, and I'm hoping it'll mean he can leave the suit of armour right away."

"Promise me you'll come and see me."

I reach out and squeeze her offered hand. "I promise."

She steers the car into the car park of the hospital. "I can't wait. How are you so calm? I'd be leaping about all over the place if it was me."

"I am, inside."

"You deserve it," she says, parking near to the maternity ward. "A happy ever after, I mean. After everything you've been through."

"Thank you, Immi. For believing me."

She shrugs and turns off the engine, but she doesn't get out of the car. "I've seen some terrible things," she murmurs, looking off into the distance. "Dark things I would never have believed could happen. Horrific murders and deaths. People can do awful things to each other.

But witchcraft is all about balance, right? I have to believe that if there's such evil in the world, there can also be an equal amount of magic and happiness."

I nod slowly, thrilled she understands. "That's what I like to think, too."

"Come on." She undoes her door. "Let's go and see what we can do for this baby."

We make our way into the hospital and go up the stairs to the maternity ward. Christian's niece is in the NICU—the neonatal intensive care unit. We wash our hands with antibacterial soap and don hospital gowns. When we go in, I see Christian standing next to the guy I saw in the pub last night, talking quietly while a woman of around my age with messy blonde hair and shadows under her eyes sits by an incubator, her gaze glued on the baby inside. There are three other incubators in the room, all flanked by parents watching them with concern.

"Hey." Christian sees us, comes over, and kisses first me, then Immi, on the cheek. "Thank you so much for coming."

"It's nothing," I say, embarrassed and suddenly fearful that I'm giving these people hope when I know I don't have anywhere near the power they need.

But I smile at Rachel and her husband, Karl, and try not to argue when Rachel whispers, "It's so kind of you to try to help us. We're so worried. Anything you can do would be marvellous."

"I'll try," I tell her, taking her hand in mine. "But I can't promise anything, okay?"

Her face is filled with hope, though, and I wish with all my heart that I'm not the one who takes it away.

"This is Cassie," she says, resting a hand on the incubator.

I look down at the tiny baby, who has a feeding tube as well as a host of other tubes emerging from her small body. I completely understand why the surgeon is hesitant to operate. How on earth do you summon the courage to cut into such a tiny body?

I clear my throat. "First of all, I brought you all something." I take the box out of the bag I'm holding and peel off the lid. It contains six chocolate muffins. "To keep your strength up," I tell them. The truth is that dark chocolate contains all the properties linked to the antidepressant effects of tryptophan, serotonin, and phenethylamine.

It has a calming, soothing effect, and I also added a spell to bring hope to carry this family through these difficult days.

Imogen has brought a flask of hot coffee and some plastic cups, and she pours one for everyone, and soon they're nibbling the muffins, their long sighs releasing the tension that's built up over the last few days for them.

Then I turn to Cassie in the incubator.

"I'm afraid we can't take her out," Rachel says sadly. "I can't even hold her. Some mother I am." Her eyes turn glassy.

Tears prick my eyes, but I force my lips into a smile and rest a hand on her shoulder. "You're doing an amazing job. Your loving thoughts for your daughter are better than any healing I can give. And anyway, the barrier makes no difference to me. Healing can pass through walls and over great distances."

I could insert my hands in the holes on the side and touch the baby, but I know that sometimes touch is stressful to an unwell new-born, so instead I rest my hands on the top of the incubator and close my eyes.

Chapter Fifteen

The others fall quiet.

It takes a while for me to stop feeling self-conscious. I know they're watching me, waiting for some amazing display, maybe a glow of light or sparkles in the air. It won't happen, of course; magic isn't like that. You can't see a spell any more than you can see someone's thoughts or feelings.

I concentrate on my breathing. In for a count of eight, out for a count of eight. I breathe from my tummy, imagining a balloon inside me, inflating, then deflating.

It's a pleasant temperature in the room, and there's a smell of lavender. Where's that from? I can't imagine it's acceptable to burn essentials oils in here. Maybe it's Rachel's perfume. But it doesn't smell like a modern perfume. It's more delicate, and reminds me of my kitchen at home, with its dried herbs hanging from the ceiling.

It also reminds me of my grandmother, Lizzie. She used to wear a lavender perfume.

"Hello, Gwen," she says.

My eyes fly open. Rachel is sitting by my side, her gaze on her daughter. Imogen is in the corner, talking to Karl and Christian in whispers. A nurse is checking the monitor of one of the other babies. The other parents are focused on their children. There's nobody else in the room.

I close my eyes again. "Gran?" I say in my mind.

"I'm here," she says. Her voice is in my head—not spoken out loud.

Emotion washes over me. "What's happening?" I ask her. "How am I hearing you?"

"When you heal, you enter the astral plane," she replies. "I can enter too, and we can meet in the middle."

"Is Mum with you?" I ask, hope swelling inside me.

"No," she says. "She's busy. It takes time after you cross to come to terms with the transition. But you'll be able to speak to her eventually."

I'm so overwhelmed, I have to work hard to keep my breathing normal. I don't want the others to think something's wrong.

"I can't stay long," she says. "I just wanted to say hello and let you know that we're watching over you."

"You and Grandad?" I ask.

"Me and Grandad, and all your other ancestors."

"Harriet and Josephine?"

"Of course. We're all here to give you strength. You're not alone."

I press my lips together, so they don't tremble. "Gran, can you help me send healing to baby Cassie? To all the babies in the room?"

"Of course I can. That's how it works, Gwen. You open yourself to the power of all the Young witches who have gone before you. Fill your heart with love and light."

So I think about Mum, and Gran, and Harriet, and Josephine. And Dad and Grandad, and the other men who've helped the witches to learn to love. I think of Imogen and Christian, and Rachel and Karl and their love for baby Cassie.

And, without meaning to, I think of Arthur, and his words, *I will just have to win you all over again.* Tomorrow I might be able to see him whole and complete. What will the future bring?

Love for my friends and family fills my heart, and I feel light flowing through me, down through my head chakra, out through my hands, flooding the room with sunshine and warmth. I know the others won't be able to see it, but I can feel it, bathing the babies and their worried parents in beautiful, healing light.

I channel it for as long as I can, enjoying the sensation, conscious of the presence of all the witches who've gone before me lending me their strength and their power. And then gradually, the light fades, and it's just me, shaky and a little sweaty, and I open my eyes.

"You okay?" Imogen asks softly. She's standing beside me—I didn't hear her come over.

I nod and lower my hands. My arms feel a little stiff. Rachel and Karl have gone, and Christian is sitting in a chair, watching us. He smiles as I look at him.

"You've been standing there for about thirty minutes," Imogen says.

"Wow. Sorry."

"No, it's fine. Rachel and Karl went to get another coffee. How do you feel?"

"A little tired. Good, though."

"Did it work?"

"We'll have to see. It takes time to work. I think what happens is that the healing gives strength and resilience and encourages the body to heal itself." I'm so tired I'm almost falling over. "Would you mind if we went home?"

"Of course not." Imogen picks up her bag and car keys. "Come on."

"Those chocolate muffins were amazing," Christian says, coming over to kiss my cheek. "Take care of yourself, Gwen."

"You too. Let me know how Cassie is, and please give Rachel and Karl my best."

"I certainly will. She wanted me to let you know, by the way, that she was sorry to hear about Liza. She met her, once, at the Italian restaurant in town, and I introduced them. They were both out for a birthday dinner and thought it was funny that they shared the same birth date."

"When is Rachel's birthday?" I ask.

"July the eighteenth," he says. "They both had cakes delivered with candles on."

Something floats through my mind like a feather on the breeze, but I'm too tired to catch it.

I watch him kiss Imogen on the cheek. "Call me," he says.

"Might do," she replies, and he gives her a wry look.

Imogen and I return to the car and drive home. I doze off on the way, exhausted from the experience. When we get home, she takes me inside, puts me on the sofa, makes me a hot water bottle and a cup of tea, then gives me a kiss and tells me to take it easy for the rest of the day. I don't need telling twice. Within five minutes, I'm asleep, and I don't wake up for a long, long time.

*

When I eventually do rouse, Merlin's lying beside me. I sit up and greet him, glad to have him there. It's mid-afternoon, somewhat gloomy and cool, rain pattering lightly on the window. I don't feel right. I guess the healing took more out of me than I realized.

I stand and stretch but can't shake the general feeling of unwellness. I feel a tad nauseous, and I have a headache. I do get migraines sometimes after doing spells, but what happened in the hospital was so positive and uplifting that I'm surprised it's had a detrimental effect. If it was that. The house feels… odd. The atmosphere is dark and heavy, something I've never felt before at home. I feel depressed and close to tears, and there's a knot in my stomach, around my solar plexus.

Frowning, conscious that sometimes negative psychic energy can feel like this, I walk around the house, checking for anything unusual. When I go into the kitchen, I feel it immediately—a dark, dragging energy, sucking all the light from the room. Merlin stands in the doorway, refusing to enter the room, barking non-stop. With shock, I stare at the big pine table in the centre. The apples and bananas in the fruit bowl look as if they're a month old—brown and oozing, covered in flies. In the sink, the flowers that Imogen bought me are dead and decaying. Gingerly, I lift the clean tea towel that rests over the batch of muffins I'd left on the worktop, and I recoil at the sight of the maggots crawling out of them.

Disgusted, I find a rubbish bag, tip the fruit, flowers, and muffins into it, and take it outside. Then I come back into the kitchen and get all my cleaning products out from under the sink. It's the festival of Ostara, so I should be spring cleaning anyway, and I set to it, ignoring the uneasy feeling in my stomach, and spending the rest of the afternoon up to my elbows in disinfectant, scrubbing every surface until the whole place gleams.

By the end of the day, I feel a whole lot better. My sickness has gone, and so has the dark, dragging feeling. Hoping to ensure it doesn't return, I light an essential oil burner and mix some lavender with tea tree and peppermint to cleanse the room, and leave it burning while I knead some dough to fill the house with the comforting smell of warm bread. By the time the light starts to fade, I'm sitting in the living room eating cheese on toast, feeling right as rain.

"So what was that about?" I ask Merlin, who's soaking up the heat from the fire. Someone had placed a curse on me; I'm certain of it. I'm not an expert in curses and prefer not to have anything to do with them, so I'm not sure quite how they did it, but it's clear that somebody meant me harm.

Was it the murderer? It wouldn't surprise me, as I already know he or she can do magic. But why come after me? What have I done?

Unbidden, I think of Matthew Hopkins and his dislike for me. Surely, he's not responsible? He couldn't be a witch and hate witches at the same time, could he?

There are no answers, so I wash up the tea things, then curl up on the sofa and settle down for an evening in front of the TV with a glass of wine. Tomorrow is Monday, and I'll be picking up the ruby. It could be the start of something big—or maybe an end, if it doesn't work. I don't want to think about that, though, so I concentrate on thinking about Arthur and hoping for the best, and put on a romcom I've seen before, but I know I'll enjoy.

Halfway through, my mobile rings. I pick it up, see Imogen's name on the screen, and answer with a smile. "Hey you."

"Hey. How are you doing? Have you recovered yet?"

I consider telling her about what happened in the kitchen, but decide not to worry her. She's got enough on her plate. "I'm feeling much better. Had some cheese on toast and now I'm having a glass of wine."

"You feel okay?"

"Umm… yes. Why?"

She hesitates for a second, although I might have imagined it. "The session at the hospital really seemed to take it out of you, that's all."

"I'm fine."

"Good. Well, I've just heard from Christian, so I wanted to tell you…" I can hear the smile in her voice. "Baby Cassie's vitals improved this afternoon, so much so that Rachel was allowed to hold her."

Joy fills me. "Oh, I'm so pleased."

"And apparently the other three babies have also shown marked improvements. You know what this means, don't you?"

"Will Cassie be able to go home soon?"

"Well, hopefully. But it means that you, Gwen Young, are an amazing woman, and I love you to the ends of the Earth. You know that, right?"

Tears prick my eyes. Goodness, I'm so emotional at the moment, and it's not even that time of the month. "Aw, Immi…"

"Christian wants to take you out to dinner to celebrate. Actually, he wants to take me out to dinner, but I refuse to take any of the credit."

I laugh and rub my nose. "You should totally go and have fun."

"I will, when we—"

"—catch the murderer, yes, I know."

"I mean it, Gwen. You truly are amazing. And you do it all with such quiet fortitude and grace. I'm so full of admiration for you."

"Oh, stop it. The baby's better because of the love of her parents and the care of her nurses. All I did was help it along a little bit."

"You can be as unassuming as you like, I still think you're wonderful. You stay safe, do you hear me? And good luck with the ruby tomorrow. Let me know as soon as you discover if it works."

"I will. Have a good evening, Immi."

"See you soon." She hangs up.

I turn off my phone and put it on the table, thinking about her last words. *You stay safe, do you hear me?* I'm sure I didn't imagine her hesitation either when she asked me if I felt all right. Did she know about the dark energy in the kitchen? And if so, how?

If she was anyone else, I might have wondered if she were somehow the cause of it, but I've known Immi most of my life, I love her to bits, and I am one hundred percent certain that even if she knew about it, she wasn't the cause of it.

But it still means someone else was.

I'm not going to be able to figure it out today, though. Baby Cassie is feeling better, and that's great news and truly something to celebrate, whether I was responsible or not. So I lift Merlin onto the sofa beside me, prop my feet on the coffee table, take a sip from the red wine, and begin to leaf through one of Harriet's Book of Shadows, while the romcom plays out cheerfully in the background.

I'm halfway through the glass of wine when I come to a page with a protection spell. My great-grandmother has written a paragraph above the instructions in her neat, slightly tilted handwriting. "There comes a time when each of us needs to think about protecting ourselves. Whether it's from a nosy neighbour, an over-zealous suitor, an aggressive co-worker, or something more sinister, there are ways a witch can protect herself from unwanted attention."

She goes on to give the ingredients of the spell. I think about Liza and the murderer, and the dark energy I felt earlier. I've often done my oatmeal cookies for protection, but I've never felt the need for anything stronger before. Now, though, I know I would feel safer if I thought I had some magical help.

So I get up, go into my nice, clean kitchen, and start collecting the various ingredients. I gather three cloves, angelica, rosemary, sage, and a pinch of salt, and place them in one of my hand-stitched cloth sachets that I sometimes use for spells and tighten the top. I then set about making the clove snaps that Harriet has suggested. I sift flour, cloves, cinnamon, butter, and salt. In another bowl I cream the butter, add egg, sugar, and orange zest, mix it all, then stir in the flour mixture until it's all combined. I knead the dough, then say the spell that Harriet prepared as I picture a protective shell around me, keeping me safe.

"Sun and moon, wind and rain, please protect this witch from pain, Goddess bless and bind this charm, keep this hedge witch free from harm."

As I roll out the dough and cut it into cookie shapes, I think about Harriet's use of the term 'hedge witch'. I tend to call myself a kitchen witch, but hedge witch or green witch are other terms for the same sort of thing—witches who work on their own, often from their kitchen, utilizing the ingredients around them to make their spells.

I put the tray in the oven and the sachet into my pocket, pour myself another glass of wine, and go back into the living room until the cookies are done. Once they've cooled, I eat a couple for my supper, and also give one to Merlin, as I figure he deserves to have some protection, too. He sneezes as he eats one, which makes me laugh—the cloves give the cookies a spicy warmth, but he still finishes it.

Well, I can't do much more than that to protect us. As we settle down for the rest of the evening, I keep the image of the protective shell in my mind, hoping it works.

Chapter Sixteen

On Monday morning, I approach the Avalon Café at around seven thirty as usual. Mackenzie's Jewellery Shop won't be open for at least another hour, but I like to get to work early so I can start baking and fill the café with warm smells before people begin coming in for their first coffee, to tempt them to buy a breakfast muffin or something for their lunch.

As soon as I round the corner, though, I can see something is wrong. The café door is open, and Delia, Cooper, Allison, and Joss are standing there talking, all looking very worried.

"Hey you," I say as I approach them. "What's up?"

"It's Sir Boss," Delia says. "He's gone."

I stop in my tracks and stare. The knight always stands just inside the doorway, as if he's welcoming customers into the café. The spot is now empty, and the only thing to mark the fact that he was ever there is the slight mark of the knight's two feet on the tiles. Merlin sniffs there, then sits down, looking forlorn.

"Did you move him?" Allison asks. "Please say you moved him."

"No, it wasn't me." My mouth has gone dry. What's happened? Has Arthur somehow managed to come to life even without the ruby? Has he just up and walked? Instinctively, though, I know that isn't the case. He's tied to the soulstone. Someone else has moved the knight.

"I know who's done this." Rage rears up inside me, and my hands curl into fists. Without another word, I turn and walk away.

"Gwen," Delia calls after me, but I don't stop. Instead, I quicken my speed and head for the centre of town. Merlin pads beside me, his step as purposeful as mine. Together, we march down to the office of the local newspaper.

The door is locked—it's not even eight o'clock yet. Inside, though, I can see a figure in the room out the back, lifting a kettle, making a cup of tea. I raise a hand and bang on the glass. "Matthew Hopkins!" I yell. "Come out and face me, you coward."

The figure inside turns, so I bang again. Eventually, he puts down the kettle and approaches the door. He studies me, smirking.

"Let me in!" I yell.

"We're not open for another thirty minutes," he points out.

"Open the door," I tell him, "or I'll break the glass and come in anyway, I swear."

"I'll call the police," he says, looking alarmed for the first time.

"You think I care about that?" I bend and pick up a large stone lying on the grass and lift it as if aiming it at the window.

"All right, all right," he mumbles. He undoes the door, opens it, and steps back.

I go inside, then turn and face him.

"You actually did it," I say, my voice little more than a whisper. "You had the suit of armour removed."

"I told you I would." He speaks mildly, with some amusement, which annoys me even more. "The knight was dangerous—that sword could have killed me."

"Knocking some sense into your thick skull is all it would have done." I stop, my chest heaving, angry and frustrated. What can coming here truly achieve? He's not going to change his mind and call the council to have them return the knight. He's won, and all he's going to do is gloat and make me feel bad about it.

"Why did you do it?" I whisper, unable to stop tears of fury and disappointment filling my eyes. "I loved that suit of armour. You know I did."

"They've moved it back to the Adventure," he says, "that's all. It belongs there anyway; I don't know what it was doing in the café. It's clearly old, and anyone could have damaged it. I truly didn't want anyone to be hurt by it."

"I don't believe you." I dash away a tear that falls. "You wanted to hurt me."

"I don't want to hurt you." He looks surprised by my declaration. "I like you, Gwen. I've asked you out to dinner enough times." His eyes darken then. "But this witchcraft thing has got to stop. It's evil and destructive, and I want to save you from yourself."

I move closer to him, unmindful of my own safety. "You know nothing about it," I say softly. "If there's anything evil and destructive in this world, it's you. Writing slanderous accusations and doing your best to cast aspersions on innocent people. I don't know how you can call yourself a human being."

"Haven't you figured it out yet?" he asks, closing the gap between us, so he's looking down into my eyes. "Every single person on this Earth is capable of harming another human being. Murderers aren't special cases. We're all evil at heart."

"I don't believe that."

"Doesn't matter. It's the truth."

I'm shaking now. "I don't care what you think. I don't believe we all begin evil. We all begin innocent, and only some of us are corrupted as we age." I refuse to believe that baby Cassie is going to have to fight against a tendency to be evil.

"You have such a fiery spirit," Matthew murmurs, his gaze caressing my face. "I know I should despise you for what you are. I know you need saving. But when I look at you, all I feel is desire…"

Before I can move, he cups the back of my head with a hand and kisses me.

Outside, I hear Merlin bark, his nails scraping at the glass, but unfortunately, I've let the door swing shut, keeping him out. I go rigid and squeal at the feel of Matthew's lips on mine, my whole body burning with resentment. I brace my hands on his chest and push, but he's strong, and he doesn't move.

At that moment, there's a loud bang and a shower of sparks, as if a firecracker has exploded between us. Matthew is thrown back, and he lands on the floor about six feet away, yelling with pain.

I don't stop to query what's happened—I turn and leg it out of the office, sprinting up the high street. With Merlin running by my side, I run until I reach the café and realize that Matthew isn't following me.

I slow to halt, breathing heavily, my mind spinning at what just happened. And then I remember—of course, the protection spell! The cookies I ate, and the sachet that's still in my jeans pocket, protected me. Harriet saved the day. Oh Goddess, what a relief.

*

The others force me to sit down, and Cooper makes me a coffee while I relate what happened, leaving out the bit about the explosion and instead substituting a knee in the groin as the reason I was able to get away.

"Only what he deserves," Delia says fervently. "What a horrible man. Are you going to report him to Imogen?"

"You know, I think I might." Imogen would love the excuse to take him in for questioning, if only to ruffle his feathers a little.

"Morning, everyone." It's Duncan coming through the door, stopping with surprise as he sees me sitting down, which I rarely do in the café as I'm always busy. "Everything all right, Gwen?"

"Matthew Hopkins stole Sir Boss and then attacked her," Cooper says rather dramatically.

"Attacked?" Duncan looks horrified.

"It's okay." I wave a hand. "I'm all right. I wasn't attacked. He tried to… you know… kiss me, that's all."

"Gwen kneed him in the nuts," Cooper adds colourfully.

"We're all very pleased about that," Delia says.

"What have you got there?" I ask Duncan in an attempt to distract everyone. I point to the large scrapbook under his arm.

"Oh, I found this in the archives." He lays it on the table. "I took it home last night to have a leaf through. It's quite interesting. It has photos of the winner of the River Brue Fishing Competition every year for the last fifty or so years." He opens the cover and shows Cooper the top photo. "Look at that perch that Brian Welch caught last year. What a beaut."

I'm not that interested in fishing, but I'm happy to be distracted for a while, plus I like anything to do with history, so I leaf through the pages, Cooper watching as he makes his father's coffee, the two of us laughing at some of the pleased expressions of the top fisherman with their magnificent catches.

"He's super proud," Cooper says, pointing to one fellow who's beaming at the camera as he holds up his fish. He looks in his late forties. A little blonde girl stands by his side, holding his hand. She must be about three years old. His daughter or his granddaughter?

I look at the description of the winner. "Henry Billingham, holding up a champion roach, 1994."

"Mm." I blink, staring at the photo. My brain's whirling, but I can't put my finger on why. I don't know the name. Why does something about the figures seem familiar?

"Crikey, it's nearly eight thirty," Cooper says. "We'd better get a move on, Gwen."

His words shake me out of my reverie, and I sigh, get to my feet, and hand the scrapbook back to Duncan.

"What are you going to do about Sir Boss?" Duncan asks.

"He's only in the Adventure," I tell him. "He hasn't gone far. I'll talk to the Council and see if I can get him moved back if I promise to sort out the dodgy right arm."

"Good," he says. "Place looks weird without him." He collects his coffee, gives us a wave, and leaves.

"I'd better get baking." I tie my apron and head out to the kitchen. "Muffins don't make themselves, you know!" I put Matthew Hopkins to the back of my mind. The man doesn't deserve any further thought.

I spend several hours kneading dough and making sausage rolls, pies, and muffins, and then around eleven, I decide I need a break. Asking Delia to hold the fort, I put on my jacket and head out. Merlin picks himself up from where he's been lazing in front of the window, and the two of us head into town.

My pulse starts to pick up as I near the sign for Mackenzie's Jewellery Shop. "What do you think?" I murmur to Merlin. "Has it worked?"

He barks and does something I've never seen him do before—a 360-degree spin. I laugh. "You're as excited as me! Come on, then. Let's see if James has worked his magic."

I go into the shop, which jangles as the door opens. Nancy, his assistant, is showing a young couple a tray of diamond rings. But James is alone, and he looks up and smiles as I approach.

"Gwen! Lovely to see you, lassie. How are you?"

"Good, thank you." My heart is beating so hard, I think it might leap out of my chest and bounce along the floor. "How did you get on with the ring?"

"It's all done, and I have to say, the ruby is one of the most beautiful stones I've ever seen." He goes out into his workshop, then returns with a small black velvet case. He pops the lid, and I get my first glimpse of Arthur's ruby ring.

The red gem is nestled in a wide gold band with a deep line running around it. It's simple and elegant.

"It's perfect," I say with delight. "Oh James, thank you so much."

He puts the price into the card reader, and I swipe my credit card. "You're very welcome, my dear. I know I shouldn't be nosy, but I have to ask, what's the name of the lucky young man for whom you've had this made?"

"His name's Arthur," I say softly, and blush.

Merlin barks, and James laughs. "Arthur, of course it is! It couldn't be anyone else here in Glastonbury. Well, I hope he likes it, lassie. You take care of it now; it's very precious."

"I will." I lean over the counter and kiss his cheek, and he laughs. "See you, James," I say.

"See ya, lassie."

I head out, my heart racing as we head back to the café. Now it's time to see if the ring works. I wonder what's going to happen?

Chapter Seventeen

I go back to the café, tell Merlin to wait outside, and then walk to the left to a large pair of double doors marking the entrance to the Adventure and go inside.

I enter the foyer and stand for a moment, looking around. The floor is covered with blue and white tiles forming a chequered pattern. Above my head is a sign that declares 'Welcome to the Arthurian Adventure!' Ahead of me on the wall is another of Beatrix's murals— a picture of King Arthur, drawing Excalibur from the stone. To my right is the reception desk where visitors buy their tickets, and then they pass through the gate and line up to wait by the side of a set of tracks for a carriage that will take them through the Adventure.

The carriages seat two or three people and move slowly along the tracks through a series of rooms that tell the story of King Arthur. These include the tale of Uther Pendragon, who wanted Igraine as his queen and how Merlin demanded their firstborn son as the price for making it happen, a huge display of the Knights of the Round Table in front of a magnificent painting of the castle of Camelot, a series of exhibits that describe the hunt for the Holy Grail, and finally an amazing tableau that depicts Arthur's death and his transportation to the Isle of Avalon.

At the end, visitors disembark from the carriages and enter an interactive museum where they can learn a little about the real Arthur, if they wish, as well as partake in a series of activities like trying to draw Excalibur from the stone, trying on a medieval helm and a chainmail shirt, firing a bow and lifting a real sword, and doing rubbings of the shields of the knights that appear on the round table in the centre of the room.

Somewhere in this building stands my suit of armour. I say mine— I know I don't technically own it, but Francis Sullivan comes into the café most days and hasn't mentioned it, and I've never had any other complaints.

There is a small queue of people waiting to get their tickets, so I stand to one side and wait for Helen Radford, one of the receptionists, to finish serving. She sees me and waves, finishes giving a young couple and their kids tickets, directs them to Gaby, who allocates visitors into the carriages, then comes over to me. Helen is in her mid-thirties, blonde and slender, fun and chatty. We have a coffee together sometimes.

"Morning, Gwen," she says. "You need something?"

"I was looking for Sir Boss," I reply. "I understand the council's health and safety department have returned him to the Adventure somewhere."

"Oh yes, that's right—Francis mentioned it this morning." Her face fills with pity. "I'm so sorry. There wasn't anything we could do about it."

"I know. I understand why they did it, but I'm going to appeal later and see if I can get him returned. It's weird without him there."

"I bet."

"So… where is he?" I'd been hoping to see him in the foyer, but there's no sign of him.

"Nathan put him in the interactive museum at the end, with the other suits." Nathan Wilkinson is the director of the Adventure.

My heart sinks. "Okay, thank you. Is it all right if I go the back way and see him?"

"Of course."

"Thanks." I leave her to serve the next customer and go over to the door marked Staff Only. I push it open, enter the corridor, and let the door close behind me.

This is like going backstage at a theatre. The corridor leads to various passageways that run behind the exhibits, so staff can come and go without being seen. It enables them to be present quickly if a naughty visitor refuses to stay inside one of the carriages, if there's a power cut, or if part of the exhibit needs fixing in an emergency. It also gives them access after the Adventure is shut, to clean up any rubbish and work on the displays.

I follow the corridor to the end and exit through the last door, letting it close quietly behind me. I'm now in the interactive museum. I've been here many times, and I walk around the edge of the room, smiling at the sight of children running around, pressing buttons on the displays, or sitting at the large round table, doing rubbings of the shields.

And then I see him, Sir Boss, lined up against the far wall along with two other suits of armour. His sword arm is chained to the wall so it can't fall on anyone. Someone's polished his armour, so he gleams as brightly as the other two knights. He looks rather splendid, actually.

I walk casually around the room and stop in front of him. I already know I'm not going to be able to free Arthur right now. There are too many people in the room and trying to get a man out of a suit of armour would definitely draw some attention. But at least I know where he is. I'll have to come back after the Adventure closes and see if I can release him then.

I slide my hand into the pocket of my jeans and close my fingers around the ruby ring. Arthur told me he was growing more conscious; is he aware of me standing here, looking at his suit of armour? Can he 'see' it?

Sighing, I go out of the final double doors and walk around the block back to the café. There seem to be so many questions and so few answers.

Merlin's waiting for me, and I fuss him up, then go in the café and through to the kitchen and decide to make something special to help prod my memory, as I'm sure I'm missing something. Allison and Joss are doing well with the lunch orders, so I pop in my earbuds, listen to some folk music, and leaf through one of my mother's journals that I brought in with me this morning. It contains some unusual recipes, and I know I spotted one for remembrance. Yes, there it is. Chocolate peanut butter ginseng cookies.

Ginseng is a plant that grows in the mountains of Eastern Asia, and its roots are well known for aiding dementia and Alzheimer's. I have it in powder form, and I make up a standard cookie mix, add chocolate chips and crunchy peanut butter for flavour as ginseng can be a little bitter, then add a teaspoon of the ginseng powder and mix it into a stiff dough.

At that point, making sure I wait until Allison and Joss are having a conversation on the other side of the kitchen, I say the spell in Alice's Book of Shadows. "In the oven, cookies bake, Goddess, let my memories awake." Hmm, that seems simple. But I know the words are irrelevant. It's all about intention, and so I close my eyes for a few seconds and picture my memory as a large library full of rooms that are gradually being unlocked.

Keeping that image in my mind, I roll the dough into balls, put them on a baking tray, and slide them into the oven.

I make a batch of muffins while I wait for the cookies to bake, then take out the tray and transfer them to a cooling rack.

Then I have a couple with a cup of tea in the break room.

After that, it's lunchtime, and I'm busy in the café, serving customers and making coffee because Cooper's at college this afternoon, and the time flies by. I don't have time to think about Arthur or the cookies or anything else in fact, and it's not until about two o'clock that the flow of customers slows down.

And it's then that something comes to me.

It happens so suddenly that I stop in the process of walking across the café, a tray of cups and plates in my hands, and stare off into the distance.

Delia looks over at me and raises her eyebrows. "You okay?"

"Yes, yes. Fine." I continue walking, but my heart's racing, and thoughts are whirling around my head.

I take the tray into the kitchen, then go into the break room and sit there for a moment.

I've remembered something. Christian told me and Imogen that on the night of the murder, he knocked over the vase standing by the front door of the library, and it rolled onto the floor. That was around five o'clock.

When I went in, at nearly six o'clock, the vase was on the table, and it held a bunch of roses.

I hadn't remembered it before, but now I recall placing my wet umbrella by the door and glancing at the roses before I proceeded through the bookstacks toward the reading room.

My head spins with everything that implies. Facts race through my head—things I've seen or heard over the past few days. And gradually, like a game of Tetris, pieces begin to slot into their rightful places.

But there are still a whole lot of things that don't make sense. Standing, I retrieve my jacket and go into the café. "Are you okay to hold the fort for a while?" I ask Delia. "I've got a few errands to run."

"Of course," she says, busy wiping down a table. "Take your time. We're all good here."

On impulse, I go over and give her a hug. "You know how much I appreciate you, don't you?" I tell her.

She laughs and hugs me back. "You're such a sweetie, Gwen Young. Off with you—go and get some fresh air."

I leave the café, collect Merlin from where he's sitting out the front, being petted and fed bits of biscuit by an elderly couple, and head down to the archaeological field unit on the other side of the library.

Leaving Merlin outside, I go into the office. I'd always hoped I'd work here one day, but it wasn't meant to be. I still enjoy coming here, though. The main room houses four desks and a large worktable in the middle. Storage rooms off to the side contain boxes of finds waiting to be cleaned and catalogued, as well as maps and documents that will eventually find their way into the library.

At the moment, Duncan and Una Richards, another of the archaeologists, are seated at the worktable, sorting through a box of what looks like a mixture of bones and pieces of wood. The box bears the words Glastonbury Lake Village, which is an Iron Age settlement on the Somerset Levels.

"Hello, Gwen," they both say as I walk up.

"Hi," I reply. "I'm sorry to disturb you, but I was wondering whether I could take another look at the scrapbook you brought in this morning, Duncan?"

"Sure," he says with surprise. Dusting off his hands, he rises, goes over to his desk, and returns with the book. "Here you go."

I place it on the table just down from them and flick through the pages until I reach the photo of Henry Billingham, holding hands with the little blonde girl. I turn it to show Duncan. "Do you know this guy?" I ask.

Duncan peers at it, then checks out the name. "No, not personally. I've heard his name at the fishing club, but that's all."

Disappointed, I show it to Una. "What about you, Una. Do you know him?"

She looks at it. "Henry? Yes. Well, knew. He's dead now."

"Oh? When did he die?"

"About... um... a year ago, I guess," she says. "Heart attack, I think."

I tap the little girl in the photo. "Is this his daughter?"

"I don't know. It doesn't look like Mary. She's got dark hair, but then I guess lots of children have blonde hair when they're born but it goes darker later."

"Mary?" I ask her, my pulse racing.

"Yes, Mary Paxton. She's his daughter. He was married to Katherine. They divorced a long time ago though, maybe twenty-five years? Katherine went back to her maiden name, Paxton, and Mary took it, too."

I stare at the photo. Una's right, some children's hair colour does change. But I can see nothing of Mary in this little girl. And the description says Henry won this competition in 1994. Mary would have been about thirteen, so she's too old, as well.

And then I realize what has been niggling at me since I saw the photo this morning. The girl in the photo has a pendant around her neck. It's a Tudor rose.

Oh. My. Goddess.

"Thank you," I tell her. "I have to be going now." I close the scrapbook. "Duncan, would it be possible for me to borrow this for a while?"

"Of course."

"Thanks. See you later."

Duncan and Una wave goodbye, and I go out, collect Merlin, then head quickly to my car.

Chapter Eighteen

I drive the short distance to the house that Liza shared with Luke. I haven't been inside, but she lost no time in telling me about it when she first bought it with him. It's much newer than mine, one of the large, expensive, detached houses on the edge of town. I don't really want to go in, especially after what Matthew Hopkins revealed on Saturday night. I'd rather have rung, but I don't want to quiz Luke about his dead wife over the phone.

I pull up outside, and get out, Merlin at my heels. I go up to the front door and ring the bell, waiting with butterflies in my stomach, both from seeing Luke and the knowledge that this is where he lived with Liza. After about thirty seconds, he answers the door.

"Oh." He looks confused. "You're the last person I thought I'd see."

"Sorry," I tell him. "I was wondering whether I could have a quick word? I won't keep you long."

"Okay." He steps back to let me in.

I hesitate, wondering whether to stay on the doorstep, then decide that would be rude and go into the house. I stop and ask, "Would you rather Merlin stay outside?"

"No, he can come in." Luke bends and ruffles the hair between the dog's ears. "Hello, boy."

Merlin doesn't growl at him, but he doesn't go starry eyed the way he does when other people scratch him, either. Although the two of them haven't met much, Merlin does seem to understand how I feel about Luke.

We walk through to the living room. Dirty plates and beer bottles rest on the coffee table. A pair of his work boots have left mud on the carpet. He sees me looking at it and shrugs. "Doesn't seem to matter now."

"I'm sorry to bother you," I say softly. "But I need to ask you a question. Can you tell me—who are Liza's parents?"

"Brenda and Colin Banks," he says without falter. "Nice enough. Gone to pieces now, obviously."

I feel a swell of confusion and disappointment. I must have been wrong. That's thrown all my assumptions into the wind.

But then he adds, "Well, adoptive parents, obviously."

I stare at him. "She was adopted?"

He nods. "Her mother died when she was four."

"What was her name?"

"Anne. She was born out of wedlock. Anne was an orphan, so when she died, Liza had nobody else to bring her up. Brenda and Colin Banks adopted her. They were very good to her, gave her everything, but they didn't know who her birth father was."

"I never knew," I murmur.

"She loved Brenda and Colin," Luke says, "but she was always very insecure about the fact that her father didn't want anything to do with her."

Liza, insecure? I would never have known. Maybe that accounts for her confidence—it was a front she conjured up to cover her insecurity.

"She was always jealous of you," Luke says softly.

"Me?" I'm astounded. "Why on earth would she be jealous of me?"

"You were always so self-assured, Gwen, even as a teen. That's why I fell for you. You might not have been the coolest girl in the school, or the prettiest, but you had this inner poise and determination that most people never achieve."

My face burns at his backhanded compliment, but I don't react. Against my hip, I'm sure I can feel the ruby ring also burning as if Arthur's expressing his indignation. Merlin sits up and glares at Luke, who doesn't notice.

"So Liza never discovered who her birth father was?" I ask, wanting to turn the conversation away from talking about us.

"Well, funny you should ask that. Just six months ago, she contacted one of those agencies who help you to find your birth parents," Luke says. "She got an email from them the day she died."

"What did it say?" My heart is in my mouth.

"I don't know. She sent me a text. She was going to tell me all about it that evening, but, well, you know what happened..." He looks sad.

"Did you tell the police all this?"

"Yes. Imogen was very interested and asked lots of questions." He frowns. "What's this about?"

I get to my feet. He's told me everything I need to know. I don't want to stay here any longer, with Luke's grief hanging in the air so thick and heavy it's palpable. There are signs of Liza all around me— her magazines still on the coffee table, her hairbrush on the mantelpiece, a pot of nail varnish on the small table beside the sofa where she must have sat in the evenings. My own grief—for Liza, despite the fact that I didn't like her much; for Luke, because I loved him once and it hurts to see him in pain; for the girl I once was who had so many hopes and dreams; for all the losses I've endured—is suddenly almost too much to bear.

"I'd better go," I tell him. "Thank you for seeing me."

"You don't have to go," he says.

"I do, Luke. I don't really want to be here. It's difficult for me to be in the home you shared with Liza. I shouldn't have come. I should have just telephoned."

He reaches out a hand to stop me. "I'm sorry if I hurt you. I didn't mean to."

It's no good; I can't hold it in any longer. "Someone told me that you started dating her two months before we broke up. Is that right?"

He stares at me. Then he drops his gaze to the floor. That very act answers my question.

"I fell in love with her, that's all," he says.

"Goodbye, Luke." I walk to the front door and go out.

"What was this all about, anyway?" he calls after me. But I'm in tears and can't answer. I run to my car, make sure Merlin's in, get in myself, and drive away.

Fighting against emotion, I try to concentrate on the details I've found out. There are still a few gaps I want to fill in before I contact Imogen. I need to speak to someone older who might have known what happened between Henry Billingham and Katherine Paxton. And there's one person I know who's a fount of information in this town.

I pull over, take out my mobile, and call Beatrix. I know she'll probably be in her art studio. Sure enough, when she answers the phone, I hear music playing in the background. I can almost see her, dressed in a white smock, a palette in her hand, smearing coloured paint across a canvas while she sings.

"Gwen!" she says. "What a lovely surprise!"

"I'm so sorry to interrupt you while you're working…"

"Not at all. What can I do for you? Are you okay?"

"I'm fine. I've just been to see Luke."

"Oh dear. Why?"

"I needed to ask him some questions about Liza. I found out something interesting, and I needed to clarify a few details. And I thought you might be able to fill in the blanks."

"I'll certainly try. Fire away."

I look at the rain pattering on the windscreen and watch it run down the glass. "It's about Henry Billingham. Did you know him?"

"I did. Nice fellow. A kind, gentle man. It was very sad when he passed away last year."

"I understand he was once married to Katherine Paxton."

"Yes, that's right. About twenty-five years ago. They divorced when Mary was thirteen or fourteen."

That would be around the time he won the fishing competition, when the photo was taken of him with a little blonde girl.

"Do you know why he and Katherine divorced?" I ask. "Was it because he had an affair?"

"That's right," Beatrix says. "It was a real scandal at the time. Apparently, he was seeing someone from Wells. A much younger woman. Katherine found out and locked him out of the house. Made a real scene—threw all his clothes out of the window, broke all his fishing rods. When he tried to talk to her she just screamed, and in the end the neighbours called the police. Mary witnessed it all, apparently. It must have been very hard for her."

"Yes, she's had a hard time, especially with Katherine's cancer."

"Katherine's what?"

"Cancer," I explain. "I spoke to Mary just before Mum died. She told me that Katherine had been diagnosed with breast cancer and didn't have long to live."

"I saw Katherine two days ago," Beatrix says. "She was talking about going on a trip to Canada in September. She seemed fine to me."

I'm so taken aback, words elude me. Katherine's not ill? So, what about the book I saw in Mary's bag?

And then I get it. Oh...

Beatrix goes quiet for a moment. "What's all this about?"

"Just trying to sort out a few things," I say. "I'm sorry to be mysterious, but I need to speak to Immi first."

"Of course, dear."

"I have to go, but I'll call you later, okay?"

"Yes, that would be lovely. Take care of yourself."

"I will. Bye." I hang up, put the car in gear, and continue driving.

By the time I get to the town centre, it's pouring down. I drive to the police station and park in the car park out the back, so I don't have far to walk. Bringing Merlin with me, and with the scrapbook tucked under my arm, I run across the tarmac to the main building and go inside.

The foyer is quiet, and the police officer sitting behind the desk is working on her computer. When I approach, she looks up and smiles. "Hello. Can I help?"

"I wondered if I could see DCI Hobbs, please," I ask.

"I'm afraid she's busy at the moment," she replies. "Can anyone else help?"

I hesitate. "I'm an old friend, and I have some very important information about a case she's working on. Could you just check to see if she'll see me?"

"Of course. Please have a seat."

I give her my name, go over to the row of seats against the wall, and sit. I've never bothered Immi at work before. Merlin sits on my foot, apparently as nervous as I am. The police officer picks up her telephone and talks quietly for a while, then hangs up. "She'll be right out," she calls to me.

"Thank you." My pulse is racing. I sit, heart racing, until the doors into the station open, and out comes Imogen.

She's wearing a dark navy suit today, her hair in a tight bun, and she looks every inch a DCI. But when she approaches me, she smiles.

"Hey," she says. "What's up, are you okay?"

"I'm fine." I moisten my lips.

"Claire said you had some information about the case," Immi says.

"That's right. I think I know who murdered Liza."

She stares at me. "Oh. Okay. Well, in that case you'd better come in."

"Shall I leave Merlin here?"

"No, he can come too. We like dogs here." She ruffles his ears, and he licks her hand.

I follow her into the interior of the station, and we walk past a large open-plan room filled with desks and whiteboards that looks like a scene out of every cop show I've ever watched. She takes me right to the end of the corridor, through a door that has 'DCI Imogen Hobbs' stencilled on the front, and into her office.

She shuts the glass door behind me and gestures to the chair on the other side of her desk.

"This is weird," I say.

"Very weird." She sits in her chair and leans on her desk. "So... where do you want to start?"

Chapter Nineteen

I take a deep breath. "I went to see Luke this morning."

"Oh?" She frowns in concern. "Did it go okay?"

"It was… difficult, but let's not talk about that. I want to talk about Liza."

"Okay."

"Luke told me that Liza was adopted."

Imogen nods slowly. "That's right. He told me the same thing."

"And on the morning she died, she received an email from the agency she'd engaged to discover her birth father. Luke didn't see the email, but I'm guessing you've managed to download it from the server, or something."

Imogen's lips curve up in a little smile. "Maybe."

"And I think it said that Liza's father was a man called Henry Billingham."

She nods slowly. "How did you figure it out?"

"Well, Henry was married to Katherine Paxton, and they had a daughter called Mary. Mary Paxton, who owns the florist."

"That's right."

"When Mary was around fourteen years old, in 1995, Henry and Katherine divorced."

"Yes."

"This was because Katherine discovered that Henry was having an affair with a woman called Anne, who came from Wells."

Imogen leans forward on the desk. "I see."

"Anne was a lot younger than he was. I think Henry first met her maybe five years before, around 1990. He fell in love with her, and she got pregnant. And obviously, they called their daughter a derivative of Elizabeth—Liza."

"Why 'obviously'?" Imogen asks.

"Think about it, Immi. Their names. Katherine and Henry. Their daughter Mary. Henry was a history buff and head of the Local History

Society. He would know that Henry the Eighth's first wife was Katherine of Aragon, and their daughter was Mary."

Imogen's eyes widen. "Of course, Bloody Mary. And his second wife…"

"Was Anne Boleyn. I imagine Henry thought it was rather funny that he married Katherine and then fell in love with Anne. And who was Anne Boleyn's daughter?"

"Queen Elizabeth the First," Immi says. "Liza."

"Yes. That's why he had the Tudor rose pendant made for Anne. Look at this photo." I show Imogen the cover of the scrapbook that explains it holds photos of the fishing competition winners and turn to the page showing the winner in 1994. "See the little girl holding Henry's hand? She's blonde, about three years old—the same age we would have been then, and she's wearing the Tudor rose pendant. It's got to be Liza."

Imogen's jaw drops. "Oh wow. You're right."

"Immi, I think that the day she died, after reading that email from the agency, Liza confronted Mary Paxton with the truth. I think Mary hated the fact that Anne broke up her parents' marriage, so the seeds for her resentment toward Liza were already sown. We may never know what happened between them, but we do know that at the end of the day, Mary came looking for Liza. I saw her waiting out by the Abbey in the dark. She must have seen her go into my café, then come out again and go into the library. She followed her in there and killed her."

"So you think Mary's the witch who cast the astrological binding spell?"

"I'm certain of it, for three reasons. Firstly, like the way I do magic with my cooking, I think she does her magic through her flowers. I think she curses the blooms sometimes. And I think you already suspected her, and that's why you bought that bouquet and gave it to me—to see if I sensed any magic on it."

She has the grace to look ashamed. "That's partly true. I did want to get you something for Ostara, and I decided to kill two birds with one stone. I'm so sorry."

I wave a hand. "I don't care. The thing is—you were right. I was very sick when we got back from the hospital, and when I went into the kitchen, the flowers had all died, and all the fruit in the bowl had rotted. I got rid of it all and felt much better, but I knew someone had cursed me."

Imogen has gone pale. "Oh no, I feel terrible. I'm so, so sorry."

"It's all right, Immi. It's a good thing—it means we're on the right track. The second reason I'm certain Mary did it is because six months ago, she came into the café and she had a book in her bag. It was called Understanding Cancer. Naturally, I assumed she or someone close to her had the disease, and when I asked her if she wanted to discuss it, she told me her mother had breast cancer and didn't have long to live. But today Beatrix told me that Katherine's planning a holiday to Canada in September, and that she seemed fine. And then I remembered the hospital."

"Baby Cassie?"

"Cassie's mum, Rachel. Christian said he'd introduced her to Liza when they were in a restaurant one evening, both celebrating their birthdays. And Rachel's birthday was July the eighteenth. The astrological star sign of Cancer. I think Mary knew that Liza was a Cancer, and she was researching the sign for the astrology binding spell. I think the tears I saw were of anger, not of pain over her mother. Right back then, she was planning to kill Liza, and she wanted to chain her to this plane, so she didn't go to heaven with Henry."

Imogen sits back in her chair. Her face is full of admiration. "That's all so amazing," she admits. "But I can't use that in court, Gwen. I need something solid to be able to convict her."

"That's where point three comes in. You know Christian said he knocked over the vase when he returned from getting his laptop from his car?"

"Yes…"

"Well, I remembered that when I came into the library to return Liza's money purse, I put my umbrella in the stand by the table, and there was a vase of roses on it."

"Roses?"

"Yes. They must have come from Mary's florist shop, and I bet if you test the vase for fingerprints, you'll discover Mary's on there."

She taps her pen on the table. "That places her at the scene. It doesn't prove she committed the murder."

I frown. "Then what about the fishing line?"

"What about it?"

"Maybe Mary knew about the photo in this scrapbook, and she used the fishing line on purpose, as a symbol." An image flares suddenly in my mind the way I thought about the roses earlier, maybe prompted by the ginseng cookies. "You need to search her shop," I tell Imogen. "There's something in there that will tie her to the case. I don't know what... sorry." I finish lamely, unsure.

Imogen smiles, playing with her pen as she surveys me. "I'll definitely look into that. I think you're right; I think she did do it."

"Is it possible for a woman to strangle someone?" I ask. "It's the only thing bothering me. I wouldn't have thought we were strong enough."

"Oh, it's definitely possible. We think she used one of the library desks for leverage as it has cuts in the top, maybe standing behind it and using her weight to pull on the line. I stole a coffee cup from the florist when Mary's back was turned. I'm hoping DNA from the cup matches that from blood spots we found at the scene which came from where the fishing line cut into her fingers. She wore gloves the next day when we saw her with Christian, remember? While I'm waiting for the results, I'll apply for a search warrant for the florists."

I sit back, relieved, and slide my hands into my pockets. My fingers close around the ruby ring. It's warm in my hand, the stone hot in its socket. As Imogen scribbles on a notepad, I close my eyes and think of Arthur.

And that's when another image pops into my mind—the bouquet of flowers that Imogen bought me from Mary's shop. Peonies, roses, tulips, freesias...

"Roses," I tell her.

She looks up and raises her eyebrows. "What?"

"In Mary's florist shop. You need to find a pot of roses. There's something buried at the bottom."

"Like what?"

"I don't know, sorry."

"Okay." She writes it down. "I'll check it out."

I blow out a long breath. "Well, I suppose I should get going. You'll let me know how you get on?"

"Of course."

We stand, and she comes around the desk. "Gwen, I truly am sorry about the curse on the flowers. I thought you might be able to pick something up from them—I really didn't think it would make you ill."

"It's okay." I give her a hug. "I know you didn't mean anything by it."

"Are you going home now?" she asks as she walks me out of the office.

"No, I'm going back to the café to help them tidy up. Then I need to go to the Adventure and sort out Sir Boss."

"What do you mean?" she asks.

I realize she doesn't know what happened this morning. "Matthew Hopkins complained to the Health and Safety Department at the Council about the fact that Sir Boss's sword nearly fell on him, and he's managed to get Sir Boss taken away."

She stops walking and stares at me. "Oh no!"

I smile. "It's okay. I'm going to talk to someone at the Council. And he's not gone far—he's only in the interactive museum part of the Adventure."

She looks around her, then leans forward and whispers conspiratorially, "Did you pick up the ring?"

"I did." I slide a hand into my jeans pocket and retrieve it. She takes it from me and turns it over in her hands.

"So he's in here, right now?" she asks, peering at the stone.

"I'm not quite sure how it works—whether he's there all the time and can hear us, or if he only becomes conscious when he's near the suit of armour. But yes, this is the ruby. And tonight, I'll find out if it's worked."

"Good luck!" She gives me back the ruby and hugs me again. "Take care of yourself." She ruffles Merlin's fur. "You too, boyo."

I blow her a kiss, and Merlin and I leave the police station and go back to the car.

I feel relieved that I've managed to get it all off my chest. It's in Imogen's hands now. I don't know if I helped much in the end, but maybe I gave her something she can work with.

The rain blows against the window as I drive back to the café. It's mid-afternoon, dark and a little blustery; I'll be glad when the clocks go forward next weekend. But inside the café it's light and warm, and I go inside with pleasure. I take Merlin through to the break room, and he curls up in his bed, where he'll stay for a few hours, sleeping soundly. Then I return to the kitchens and get to work.

The hours pass quickly as I make muffins and coffees, deliver them to customers, and then begin to clear up for the day. As six o'clock draws near, Delia and I wipe down the tables, and then after she's gone, I sweep the floor and wipe over the counter.

It's weird being here without Sir Boss by the door. I haven't had time today, but tomorrow I'll ring the Council and see if I can speak to someone about getting permission to have him returned. In the meantime, though, it's time to see if I can bring Arthur to life.

I turn off the lights, and Merlin and I go out into the dark evening. I lock the café, then walk the short distance to the entrance to the Adventure. Briefly, I stop and remove my earrings, slipping them into my jacket pocket, then I continue. The doors are locked, but I tap on the window, and Helen, who's just finishing up, comes over with a smile and lets me in.

"So sorry," I tell her, "but I've lost one of my earrings." I bring out one of the pair I was wearing from my pocket and show her. "It looks like this—I don't suppose it's been handed in?"

Her face creases with concern. "No, sorry."

"Oh, that's a shame. I have a feeling it came out in the interactive museum area. I don't suppose I could quickly go through and check? They belonged to Mum, and they're quite precious to me." I try not to feel guilty about lying.

"Of course," she says. "I'm going shortly, but you can let yourself out of the south entrance. The cleaners have just started in the Uther room—they'll lock up after you."

"Thanks, Helen. You don't mind if I take Merlin with me?"

"No of course. He's a good boy."

I smile and go through the doors marked Staff Entrance into the corridor. The automatic lighting pops on, guiding me along the quiet passageway. Now the Adventure is closed, there's no rumbling of the carriages along the tracks, no excited squeals of children or conversation amongst the adults. A vacuum cleaner hums on the other side. It's eerily quiet, and my pulse, which was already speeding up with my excitement, is now racing.

I exit the corridor at the end and enter the interactive museum. The room is semi-dark, and I can just about make out the suits of armour on the other side. I could turn on the lights, but I leave them off, conscious of the security camera in the corner. I can't do much about that; I can only hope that nobody thinks to checks the tapes and sees what happens here tonight.

Sir Boss stands between the other two knights, silent and stern. Merlin sits beside him, watching me expectantly. I extract the ruby ring from my jeans pocket, take a deep breath, and lift the helm's visor.

Chapter Twenty

"Good evening," Arthur says.

I squeal at the sight of his blue eyes in the helm, then burst out laughing. "Wow, you made me jump!"

"Sorry." He smiles. "It's nice to see you again."

"It's nice to see you, too." Thankfulness floods my heart. I hadn't realized until this moment how much I'd feared I wouldn't be able to get him back. "How are you?"

"I'm fine," he says. He looks down at the ring in my hand. "You managed it, then."

"Yes. Where have you… you know… been?" I ask. "Did you stay with the ring, or were you in the suit of armour?"

"I stayed with the ruby," he says. Then he glances around the room. "Where am I?"

"Matthew Hopkins got the Council to move you. I'm not happy about it."

He chuckles. "I bet you're not."

"Sir Boss has stood in the café as long as I can remember."

"Are you still going to call me Sir Boss when I'm free?"

I laugh. "Sir Boss is the name of the suit of armour."

"I don't mind," he says. "I quite like the title."

"Stop teasing me. I'm busy." I study the metal plates of the suit. I'm not quite sure how this is going to work. The plates are joined by leather straps. Do I need to take off all the plates one by one?

"Maybe start with the gauntlet," he says.

He wants me to put the ring on him. I can understand that. In the semi-darkness of the room, I bend and look at the left gauntlet. It's surprisingly intricate. Steel plates are attached to a thick leather glove that looks a bit like a gardening glove, each plate overlapping with the next so the knight can bend his fingers to hold his sword or a horse's reins. Two leather straps with buckles ensure the glove doesn't slide off the owner's hand.

I begin by sliding the straps through the buckles. Once they're undone, I take the gauntlet in my hands and gently pull. It slides off easily. And there beneath it is a strong hand with clean square nails and a light dusting of brown hair.

"Oh," I say, shocked to finally see him. He flexes his fingers, tightening them into a fist, then splaying them wide, but he doesn't say anything.

My own hand is shaking now, as I take the ruby ring and try it on his hand. It's too small for his third and fourth digits, but it fits snugly onto his little finger, and once it's there, it looks as if it couldn't have gone anywhere else.

Behind me, Merlin barks.

I smile, thinking he's barking at the fact that Arthur's finally wearing the ruby ring, but within a few seconds I turn with concern, conscious that his rapid barks are a warning. I inhale sharply as I see that someone has exited the passageway behind me and is standing on the other side of the room.

It's Mary Paxton.

I straighten, my heart pounding.

She looks up at the corner of the room, where the security camera is watching us. Out of her pocket, she takes a handful of powder, holds it in the palm of her hand, and blows on it. It dissipates through the room in seconds and forms a mist above our head, obscuring us from the sight of anyone watching the scene. Oh… that's serious magic.

"Hello, Gwen," she says, walking into the room. She starts circling the round table, coming toward me. Her salt-and-pepper hair is limp from the rain. Her raincoat is hanging open, and her clothing is wet. Her eyes look a little crazy, and she's breathing heavily.

"Mary." My head is spinning. Has she come to do me harm?

She glances around. "What are you doing in here?"

So she didn't see me talking to Arthur. Not wanting her to see his bare hand or his eyes, I move away from the suit of armour toward the exit, and she turns to follow me.

"Stop," she demands, and I stop moving.

"I came to find an earring I dropped," I tell her, pleased that my voice sounds calm. I take out the one I showed Helen and hold it up. "I visited the museum earlier, and I'm sure I left it in here."

She nods slowly, already losing interest. "Well I'm glad I got you on your own," she says. "I figured it's time we had a little talk."

I lift my chin, determined not to show her how scared I am. "What about?"

"I think you know what about," she says softly. "Mum rang to tell me that Imogen Hobbs and the rest of her oafish officers are currently traipsing through my shop with their filthy boots."

So Imogen must have got her search warrant. *Hurry up, Immi*, I think in my mind. *I need help!*

"Why are they doing that?" I ask.

"Stop playing dumb," she snaps, "it doesn't suit you. You know perfectly well what they're doing. You sent them there. It's all your fault. Mum heard Imogen talking to her sergeant, and she said the idea of looking in the shed was yours."

I don't say anything, mainly because I know there's nothing I can say that will make Mary believe I'm not involved in this.

"They won't find it," she says. "I've hidden it well."

"Hidden what well, Mary?" I hold her gaze, as the final piece of the puzzle comes to my mind. "Do you mean Liza's Tudor rose pendant? I don't think you've hidden it as well as you thought."

She stares at me. "What do you mean?"

"It's at the bottom of a pot of roses, isn't it?"

Her cheeks pale. "How did you know that?" she whispers.

"Magic," I tell her. "Obviously. As one witch to another, you should have realized that."

Her hands tighten into fists by her side. I glance down at them, and a cold sliver of ice runs down my spine as I see a coil of fishing line in her right hand.

"You don't need to do this," I tell her, my heart banging against my ribs.

"Oh, I think I do. If they can't find the pendant, they won't be able to pin Liza's death on me."

"They will," I tell her. "I've already told Immi to look under the roses. She's found drops of blood from your hands at the scene of Liza's murder. And you made the mistake of placing the roses in the vase that Christian knocked over at the entrance to the library before you killed her. I saw them, and it places you at the scene of the crime."

Her face is now a strange purple colour. "You think you're so smart," she says, her voice hoarse with emotion. "Meddling like an old woman."

"That's me," I tell her, edging toward the exit. "Old and crotchety."

"Trying to make Christian love you with your cookies and muffins," she says.

"Christian?" I stop walking, surprised. "What do you mean? I don't like Christian in that way."

"Of course you do." She spits out the words as if they're bitter pills. "You're all over him with your red hair and your innocent smile. You're just the same as Liza, batting her eyelashes at him like a trollop."

"Liza?" Now I'm confused. "Liza was married to Luke."

"She wanted Christian," Mary snaps.

"Mary, you're wrong…"

"Don't tell me what I am!" She's clearly losing the plot.

I'm sure Liza wasn't interested in Christian. She might have been many things, but as far as I know she never cheated on Luke, and they were happy together.

Mary's obviously developed an unhealthy obsession for him, and it's clouding any common sense she might once have possessed.

"Christian's only interested in one person," I tell her gently. "Imogen. They both like one another, and it won't be long before they start dating properly."

"You're wrong!" She screams the words.

"I'm not, Mary, and—"

"Stop it! Shut up, shut up!" And she lunges for me, her hands raised to bring the fishing line around my neck.

The next ten seconds pass in a blur of action as several things happen at once. Merlin leaps for her, and his jaws close around her arm. She screams and hits out at the dog, sending him flying across the tiles. Fury fills me at the thought that she might have hurt him, and I step forward to do something—I don't know what, hit her, maybe, although I've never punched anyone in my life.

But before I can reach her, my knight in shining armour comes to the rescue again. Arthur tears himself from the stand, wrenching the chain out of the wall where it held up his sword arm, and he walks forward, lowering his arm so his sword is pointing at Mary.

Her jaw drops at the sight of the knight coming to life. She lifts a hand to press against her mouth as she screams, backing away until she meets the round table, and for a moment I think she's going to have a heart attack, because her face is filled with horror.

Then behind me there's a crash as the south door flies open, and Imogen comes bursting in, half a dozen officers hot on her heels.

She glances at the knight and her eyes widen, but she doesn't stop, instead going straight up to Mary, and she quickly pulls Mary's arms behind her back and fastens a pair of handcuffs on her as one of the officers switches on the lights.

"Immi!" I'm so relieved I nearly pass out.

"Mary Paxton, I'm arresting you for the murder of Liza Banks in the library on the night of the seventeenth of March," she declares. "You do not have to say anything. But it may harm your defence if you do not mention when questioned something which you later rely on in court. Anything you do say may be given in evidence."

She finally looks at me. "You were right," she says. "We found the Tudor rose locket at the bottom of a pot of roses. And the DNA test has come back from the blood spots at the library, and it matches the DNA from the coffee cup."

"It was only partly about Henry being Liza's father," I tell Immi. "Mary was in love with Christian, and she thought Liza also wanted to date him."

"Christian?" Imogen stares at her. "My Christian?"

I wait for Mary to do something awful—to spit at her, or to give her a mouthful of foul language, but instead she looks forlorn, and tears start rolling down her face. I can't help but feel a stab of pity. I know what it's like to be lonely. Mary's love turned into an unhealthy obsession, but she's not necessarily to blame for that. We can't always help our feelings.

Imogen looks around, and I finally remember that we're not alone. One of the officers is bending talking to Merlin.

"Is he okay?" I ask.

"He's fine, aren't you, fella?" The officer ruffles the dog's hair, and Merlin licks his face.

Imogen's gaze slides to the suit of armour beside me. "And what's going on here?" she asks softly.

I look at the knight. Arthur lifts his left arm and raises his visor. The ruby glints in the light. "Hello," he says.

I clear my throat. "This is Arthur." Conscious of the other officers looking at him curiously, I add, "He's a friend of mine. He helps out with the museum, and he was trying on the suit of armour to see if it fit when Mary came in."

Mary stares up at him as if she knows that's not what happened, but she doesn't say anything.

"I see," Imogen says. She extends her right hand to him. "Hello, Arthur."

He leans his sword against the round table. Then, with his left hand, he unbuckles the straps on his right gauntlet and slides it off. Finally, he shakes her hand. "Nice to meet you at last," he says.

He releases her hand, and we both watch as he undoes the catch holding on his helm and lifts it off. I stare up at him, knowing I'm blushing as his warm blue eyes smile down at me.

"Well, I'd better get Mary off to the station," Imogen says. "Maybe the two of you would be kind enough to come in first thing tomorrow, and I'll take a statement."

"Of course," I say, and Arthur nods.

"Okay." She gives me a final, amused look, then steers Mary out of the building. The officers follow, leaving Arthur with Merlin and me.

I let out a long, relieved sigh, then turn back to Arthur. He's watching me, and he smiles.

"You saved me again," I tell him.

"Getting to be a habit," he replies. He tips his head to the side and studies me with gentle concern. "How are you?"

I inhale deeply, then let out a long, shaky sigh. "I'm okay."

"Are you sure?"

I bend and put my arms around Merlin. "I am now I know you're both okay." I kiss Merlin's ears. "I was so worried about you," I whisper. "Thank you for trying to save me."

Merlin whines and kisses me back. I smile and ruffle his ears, then straighten to look at the man standing beside me.

We look at each other for a long, long time.

"You're really here," I say eventually.

"Looks like it." He lifts the hand with the ruby ring and looks at it, then flexes his hand again. "So… are you ready to help me out of this suit?"

Chapter Twenty-One

I study Arthur suspiciously. "Are you wearing anything under the armour?"

His eyes twinkle. "You'll have to find out."

"Arthur..."

"Yes, Gwen. I'm wearing what a medieval knight would wear. I'm very authentic."

Grumbling under my breath, I begin to undress him.

Over the years, I've read a lot about medieval armour, so I know the names of the various plates, and I have an idea of how they go on him.

His gauntlets are already off, so I decide to continue with his arms. I undo the straps holding on the couters or elbow plates, then the vambraces or lower arm guards. He seems to be wearing a long-sleeved gambeson beneath the armour—it's a quilted cloth jacket, probably stuffed with animal hair. No wonder he complained he was hot.

Next, I undo the tassets, which are plates that protect the upper thighs, then I remove the faulds, which cover a knight's waist and hips. After this I take off the plackart, which is the plate that covers the lower half of his torso at the front, the pauldrons on his shoulders, and the large breastplate, from which the modern bullet-proof vest is descended. After removing the back plate, I take off the spaulders that protect his shoulders and the gorget that covers his throat.

Determined not to be distracted by his broad shoulders and the fact that he's a man and definitely real, I remove the cuisses or thigh plates, the poleyns that protect his knees, the greaves that cover his shins, and finally the sabatons that cover his feet.

I work quietly, concentrating on the items, the buckles and straps, and Arthur doesn't speak either. Once, when I remove the sabatons, he leans on my shoulder for balance as I kneel by his feet, and I have to fight not to giggle. I think I'm a little hysterical from all the drama tonight. I feel a bit lightheaded too. I need something to eat.

When I've removed all the plates, I unlace the padded gambeson, and he bends forward so I can pull it over his head. I have to tug it hard, but eventually it comes off, bringing his linen top halfway off with it.

I stare as he straightens, the top taking a moment or two before it falls back down. Oh Goddess. His torso is amazing. Even his muscles have muscles.

I step back and take in the full picture. He's tall, maybe six two, and broad shouldered, with muscular arms that demonstrate the years he must have spent wielding a sword and fighting in battle. The woollen trousers he's wearing also cling to muscular thighs. He's barefoot, and his jaw and cheeks show a few days' worth of stubble.

It's King Arthur. Here, in the flesh.

What do I do now?

His blue eyes turned my insides to caramel, but I need to stay practical. "We should get you home," I tell him. "You can have a shower and I'll ask a friend to bring you round some clean clothes." Uncle Max won't mind parting with a few items. "And then you should have something to eat."

"I have to admit, I'm ravenous," he says, rubbing his stomach in a circle. "It's an unusual feeling. I haven't been hungry for fifteen hundred years." He drops his hand. "But there are two things we have to do first."

"Okay."

"We should put Sir Boss back together," he says.

I look at the pieces of armour strewn about the floor. "Oh, yes, I suppose so."

"It won't take long. I'll help."

We start reassembling the knight on the stand. Arthur's right: it's easy now I know what bit is attached to what, and within ten minutes the knight looks as good as new.

The only issue is that Arthur yanked the chain out of the wall that holds up the knight's sword arm.

"Sorry about that," he says.

"It's okay, I'll talk to Nathan about it tomorrow. We'll stick with the story about you trying on the armour," I tell him.

I step back from the knight. "You said there were two things we have to do?"

"Yes. Can you take me through to the library?"

My eyebrows rise. "Um… yes, of course. There's a staff-only door that'll take us through."

I lead him across the room to the door, and we go through into the dimly lit passageway. This time, instead of heading back to the foyer, I turn right, and we emerge in the corridor leading to the museum and library offices.

Hoping we don't bump into anyone, as I'm not ready to explain Arthur's presence yet, I lead him into the library's reading room. It's dark and quiet; it closes at six most evenings.

"This is where Liza died," he says, standing in the middle of the room. The tape marking her body has now gone, but he's right over the spot where I found her.

"Yes." I'm puzzled as to why he wanted to come here.

He glances around, then takes my hand and leads me to one side. "Stand here," he instructs.

Trying not to blush at the feel of my hand in his, I do as he bids and wait as he returns to the centre of the room. What's this about?

To my surprise, Merlin goes with him, as if he's aware what Arthur is about to do. The dog sits by his side, as Arthur dips his head and closes his eyes.

For about thirty seconds, nothing happens. Merlin sits quietly, and I have the oddest feeling he's concentrating, too. I don't move, willing to wait until Arthur tells me to move.

And then, between us, a shape begins to form. At first, it's just a sort of glittery dust, as if it's a scene out of *Star Trek* and someone's transporting from the Enterprise. Gradually, it turns into a person.

It's Liza.

I hold my breath. She turns her head and looks at me. Her eyes glimmer with tears. "Thank you," she mouths.

I can't speak; I'm so full of emotion. I watch as Arthur stretches out his arms and turns his hands palms up. Merlin stands and faces him. Around the room, the twelve astrological symbols suddenly appear as gold glittery magic on the tiles. Capricorn, Aquarius, Pisces, Aries… they lift and evaporate, the glitter dispersing into the air.

The last to go is the two arcs ending in circles—the sign of Cancer. It brightens, shining so much that I have to look away, and for a moment, I'm certain I can hear singing.

Then, slowly, the brightness dims and returns to normal. The symbols have gone.

I look back. Liza has vanished.

Merlin shakes himself, then sneezes.

"Where's she gone?" My whisper sounds loud in the quiet library.

Arthur lowers his arms and opens his eyes. "To where she should have been all along."

"Heaven?"

He smiles.

I walk toward him and stop a few feet away. "How did you know how to release her?" I ask.

"Someone told me."

"Who?"

He looks at the Labradoodle sitting in front of us.

"You're kidding," I say.

He just smiles again. I glare at Merlin. "I knew you were psychic!" I say, and Arthur laughs.

I study his face, his glowing blue eyes. "Are you an angel?"

He shakes his head.

"But you have a connection to them," I murmur. "You're part of their world."

He doesn't reply; he just gives me a look that says *Sorry, I don't know.*

Merlin stands and pads around the room, sniffing the floor. We watch him, then look back at each other. Arthur holds up his hand, examining the ruby ring.

"Thank you for doing this," he says.

"You're welcome."

He lowers his hand. "I know it cost you lots of money."

I shrug. "It had to be done."

"It didn't. You could have sold the ruby."

I frown. "I would never have done that."

"No," he says softly, taking a few steps closer to me, until we're only a foot apart. "I know." He lifts a hand and tucks a stray strand of hair behind my ear. "Your soul is almost as beautiful as the rest of you." He smiles.

I blush, remembering what Luke said earlier this morning: *You might not have been the coolest girl in the school, or the prettiest, but you had this inner poise and determination that most people never achieve.*

"You think I'm beautiful?" I say, knowing I'm searching for compliments, but so filled with hope it's hard to hold it in.

"The most beautiful girl I've ever seen," he says, cupping my cheek.

For a moment, I think he's going to kiss me. Part of me wants him to. Even though we haven't known each other long, I feel as if I've known him my whole life—well, lives, if I am the reincarnation of his queen. *The wife I adored, and who adored me,* he once told me. *I will just have to win you all over again.*

But I have to be careful. I want to believe in happily ever afters, but this is the real world, not a movie, and as a woman, I can't throw myself into every situation without regard for my physical and emotional safety.

I think he reads my wariness in my eyes, because he doesn't kiss me. He slowly lowers his hand, and just gives me a gentle smile.

I should walk away, put some distance between us. But then I think of Liza, and of Luke, sitting in their house alone, in the dark, missing her. I think of Mary, crying in her cell, and the way she obsessed over Christian, who will never return her feelings. I think of Imogen—the way she blushes when she looks at Christian, and the fact that hopefully they have a lifetime of discovering each other, and of being happy together.

I move forward, slide my arms around Arthur's waist, and rest my cheek on his broad chest. And he doesn't laugh or mock me. Instead, his arms come up to hug me, and we stand like that for a very long time, while Merlin comes to sit beside us, and sighs.

A Knight on the Town (The Avalon Café Book 2)

A good knight out is always welcome...

When kitchen witch Gwen Young releases King Arthur from the suit of armour in her café, it's just the beginning of a new adventure, as he accompanies her out on the town, discovering his new world and helping her solve another murder.

Now available on Amazon!

*

Join the Avalon Café Readers!

Want to know when the next Avalon Café story is available? Join my mailing list to stay informed, and you'll also be able to download a free, exclusive short story (not for sale) about how Gwen met Merlin! Go to my website for more details:

Website: http://www.hermionemoon.com

About the Author

Hermione Moon writes cozy witch mysteries with a sprinkling of romance, set in Glastonbury, England. She also writes steamy contemporary romance as Serenity Woods, and is a USA Today bestselling author under that name. She currently lives with her husband in New Zealand.

Website: http://www.hermionemoon.com

Facebook: https://www.facebook.com/hermionemoonauthor

Made in the USA
Monee, IL
26 May 2020